Napier's Bones

Greg Michaelson

Copyright © 2017 Greg Michaelson
All rights reserved.
ISBN: 1973703521
ISBN-13: 978-1973703525

All characters are fictional, and any resemblance to anyone living or dead is accidental.

A McStorytellers publication

http://www.mcstorytellers.com

Greg Michaelson lives and works in Edinburgh. His first novel, *The Wave Singer* (Argyll, 2008) was shortlisted for a Scottish Arts Council/Scottish Mortgage Trust First Book Award. The book received much praise:

"Michaelson's debut is an intriguing Bildungsroman set on the shores of a post-apocalyptic Scotland." – Mark Lambert, *Scotland on Sunday*

"PAPERBACK OF THE WEEK... It's a future society that feels very different from our own, and, thanks to Michaelson's consistency and attention to detail, is highly convincing." – Alastair Mabbat, *The Herald*

"Big wave coming: Computer scientist and old-leftist Greg Michaelson's first novel takes place after the end of civilisation ... but he reckons there could be a silver lining." – Colin Waters, *Sunday Herald*

"There is another side to irrevocable change. And it is worked out in innovative science fiction such as Naomi Mitchison's *Memoirs of a Spacewoman*, Iain M. Banks's *Culture* and Greg Michaelson's *The Wave Singer*." – Caroline McCracken-Fisher in Scotland as Science Fiction, *Bucknel University Press*

Contents

1. In the shop	6
2. On the border	21
3. In the cell	40
4. On the hill	60
5. In the museum	77
6. Sur la plage	92
7. In transit	108
8. In the village	126
9. On the strand	146
10. In the crypt	164
11. On the bench	184
Appendix 1	204
Appendix 2	208
Acknowledgements	212

Ring-a-ring o' roses,
A pocket full of posies.
A-tishoo! A-tishoo!
We all fall down.

1. In the shop

I should have found the body, it was my turn to clean upstairs but I was late cashing up and Robin said she didn't mind doing it.

OK, Robin's my boss. She was my friend first, though. At least I thought she was. Robin runs the bookshop where I work. Because it's a radical bookshop, we like to pretend we're equal. But it's her bookshop, really.

The body was still warm. A middle-aged man. Face down. Nondescript grey suit and black raincoat. White shirt. Stripy tie, maybe a club. Clean brown shoes. Always a bad sign.

"Do you recognise him?" said Robin.
"Never seen him before." said I. "Shall we call the police?"
"Better check the pockets first," said Robin.

Left coat pocket: car keys - VW; half empty tin of small cigars.
Right coat pocket: calf leather driving gloves.
Left jacket pocket: empty.
Right jacket pocket: empty.
Right trouser pocket: snotty handkerchief.

"Right handed," said I.

Left trouser pocket: nothing.

"No matches or lighter?" said I.
"Check the inside pocket," said Robin.

Personal organiser - expensive; Japanese; colour screen; infra-red link.

"Bound to be PC or Mac compatible," said Robin. "Let's upload it."

No addresses or phone numbers. No appointments. No birthdays. No bill reminders. Just one file. Six bytes long. Password locked. Encrypted.

"Shall we call the police now?" I asked again.
"Try the car next," said Robin. "Must be nearby".

Outside. Blue. This year's registration number. I wrote it down while Robin opened the doors.

Nothing on the seats.
Nothing in the door wells or the glove compartment.
Nothing in the ash tray.
Empty boot.

"He can't hurt us," said Robin, locking the driver's door. "You call the police while I stick the organiser back."
"We better wipe everything down first," said I.

The police arrived before I'd put down the phone, the ambulance hard behind.

"Bloody lefties," said the Sergeant, as they cordoned off the shop. "What's he done then, blown himself up with his own bomb? They should shut people like you down."

Robin and I watched from the pavement. They interviewed us half-heartedly but we'd nothing to say.

"No signs of violence," said the police surgeon, as they brought out the bulging body bag. "Probably a heart attack. You both sure you didn't touch anything?"

"Always best to ignore the bastards," said Robin, as the ambulance groaned up the hill. "You know they'll close us down given half a chance."
"I'll put up the shutter," said I.
"Don't forget to clear all that stuff from our system," said Robin.
"Shit!" said I.
"What's the problem?" said Robin.
"These organisers," said I. "When you download them they delete everything automatically. Saves power. You upload it all again when you've finished working with a decent size screen and keyboard."
"Hope no one notices," said Robin.
"I'll send myself that file," said I. "Just to be on the safe side."

I stopped by the chip shop on the way home. They used to say fish was brain food but it hasn't done cats much good.

The flat is what's known as a main door. That is, it's at ground level with the front door letting directly onto a tiny garden perpetually full of crisp packets and pizza boxes and beer cans.

I ate the fish supper and tossed the brown paper into the waste paper basket. I then turned on the mighty Wurlitzer, worked out how much email I could afford to read and pulled across the file.

Six bytes. Sounds small doesn't it. Two to the forty eight possibilities. Might as well try and disentangle the eggs from an omelette.

Instead I fired up Multi-User Mindwarp. I must have played for four hours straight before finally dozing off. When I woke up at four a.m. the modem lights were still winking.

Scottish Telecom'll lose a fortune if they ever go for connection charges instead of metered data. I powered down and went to bed.

When I got to the shop next morning, the shutter was on the pavement and there was a hole where the front window had been. The shop computer system was gone. The police weren't interested. Nor were the insurance company. Robin was cheerfully stoical.

I didn't feel so good. Runny nose. Sore throat.

A quiet morning. Not many browsers. The emergency glazier fitted new glass in the window. The distributor's van dropped off a box of Booker shortlist.

Around lunchtime, the Professor came in. You can tell academics a mile off because they always wear what was fashionable when they were undergraduates and couldn't afford it. The Professor was no different. Around forty-five. Doc Marten's. Levi 501's. Check shirt. Black leather jacket, thirties's motor cycle cop cut.

OK, the Professor's my best friend. I was his best man. And I witnessed his divorce. But that's in the future. Or the past. The Professor can't stand Robin. Robin forgives him.

"Bit of a mess," said the Professor, scanning the shambles. "Any sign of my order?"
"Hard to tell without the machine," said I.

"You could always look on the shelves," said the Professor.

I scoured the back room and returned empty handed to the front desk where the Professor was grazing the new book stack.

"Nothing, I'm afraid," said I.
"Any clues who took it?" asked the Professor, nodding towards the forlorn mouse on the empty foot print.

Repetition becomes tiresome.

"... so all we've got to go on is the secure file," I finished laconically. "Oh, and a box of cigars. Do you fancy one?"
"Don't mind if I do," said the Professor.
We stepped out of the gloom onto the pavement.
"Got any matches?" said I.
"Jaunty alummette," said the Professor, proffering the Zippo.

I opened the tin. A piece of card fell out. The Professor bent over and retrieved it.

"'Napier's bones'?" he read.
"Maybe it's the password?" said I.
"Too long," said the Professor. "Ten characters maximum on that model. Where's that cigar then?"
"Only two left," said I. "Have one."
"Thanks," said the Professor, turning away from the wind whistling up the cobbled hill.

We stood and smoked in silence. A steady stream of cars and tourists passed up and down the Row.

"Well," said the Professor, dropping the butt down the gutter grating. "If you send me the file I'll have a go at it."

"How are you going to do that?" asked I. "We don't know anything about him."

"Oh don't believe all that rubbish about people using their birthdays or telephone numbers or cats' names or mistresses vital statistics as passwords," said the Professor. "This smells professional. Nothing for it but monkeys and typewriters."

"You can't try all the combinations," said I.

"I can't" said the Professor. "Drop by the lab after you close?"

"OK," said I.

I sneezed as I re-entered the shop.

A customer was waiting by desk. I was sure I'd never seen him before but he looked curiously familiar, in an uncanny sort of way.

"Nasty cold," said the customer.

"Can I help you?" said I.

"Had it long?" asked the customer.

"Just crept up on me," said I.

The customer looked me hard in the eyes.

"Napier's bones," he said softly.

"Is there a problem?" asked Robin pushing her way between us to dump the pile on the desk. "Good thing we keep paper records. Could you collate this lot, please?"

I made for the door but the customer was gone.

The one o'clock gun from the Castle shook the new window pane. I went up the hill to the sandwich bar. A cluster of children surrounded the cast iron statue of Greyfriars Bobby, their teacher watching them nervously.

"The usual?" said Phil, behind the counter.
"The usual," said I.
"Minestrone?" said Phil putting an egg mayonnaise with cucumber on rye, and a ham and tomato on wholemeal, into brown paper bags.
"At least it's not oxtail", said I, proffering a £10 coin.

A quiet afternoon. Not many browsers. Around six p.m. Robin emerged from the back room.

"We might as well shut up shop," she said. "Maybe it'll be busier the morn'. Do you want to clean upstairs today?"

The sunset was deep red over the Castle as I crossed the road and walked down into the Grassmarket. The University still had premises between the graveyard and the gaunt grey walls of the derelicts' hostels. I went up the close, through the archway into the courtyard, past the beam engine and into the crumbling 1930's School of Mines building.

In the Professor's lab, the monkeys had hung up their bananas and the typewriters had morphed into workstations. I logged across to my home machine and sent the Professor a copy of the email from the shop.

OK, I used to work in the University, way before everything went to pieces. The Professor lets me keep my login.

"Right!" said the Professor. "Six p.m. So it's four a.m. on the east coast of Australia. Lots of idle name servers."
"How do they help?" said I.

There are two ways in which technical activities may be described. Neither is satisfactory. The Socratic dialogue tends to sophist's choice but a succinct account simultaneously bores experts and distracts from neophyte plot engagement.

"Well," said the Professor, "every local computer network has a name server which can work out where to route email. Every name server has a fire wall process to stop people from outside getting back through to that local system. But the international networking standard was developed originally for the American military. So the US government insists that every name server must recognise a secret address which will give them limited access beyond the firewall. Of course, they change the secret addresses randomly all the time. They claim it's to monitor criminal use. I guess it depends on your idea of criminal. Anyway, if you monitor the network yourself, you can spot when the secret address changes and you've a short time in which you can use it to run a small program on any other name server."

"So how do you monitor the network," said I, after a decent interval.
"None of your heroic hacking," said the Professor. "Put a junction on the cable between your own system and the outside world. A bit like liberating electricity, don't you remember?"
"Oh yes," said I. "If it's so easy, why doesn't everyone do it?"
"It isn't," said the Professor. "They don't."
"How long will it take to break the code?" said I.
"Usually some time between now and the heat death of the universe," said the Professor. "But with a tiny file like this, not more than a couple of weeks."
"Won't anyone notice?" said I.
"Probably," said the Professor. "Anyway, what I'll do is run the code cracker on all the Australian name servers. They'll send me back any solutions where 85% of the text gets through a spelling and grammar checker. I'll then look at the stuff as it comes in."
"Won't there be loads of solutions?" said I.

"Tons," said the Professor. "And we don't even know if it's in English."

While the Professor set up his fiendish experiment, I surfed listlessly. Endless links between self-indulgent non-sequiteurs. Reading's never been so popular. At least the old encyclopaedias had coherent ideologies and attractive bindings.

"Off they go!" said the Professor, closing down the screen manager. "Fancy a pint?"
"I've a lousy cold," said I.
"Hair of the dog!" said the Professor brightly. "My shout."

The Professor chained up the wrought iron gates across the courtyard. We crossed the road and entered the Last Drop. The city gallows used to stand in the Grassmarket and several local pubs commemorate its victims. The Professor approached the bar and felt theatrically in his pockets.

"Could you lend me a fifty 'til I can get to a machine?" he asked.
"There's one just over the road," said I.

The Professor shambled off. I paid for the drinks and took them over to an empty table by the window. As I took a long pull at my pint, the Professor returned, brandishing a fist full of pounds.

"So how's it going," I said, wiping foam from the tip of my nose.
"The bitch is taking me to the cleaners," said the Professor, sitting down opposite me.
"Dog eat dog," said I. "What did you expect?"
"Well of course she's right!" said the Professor. "I transgressed, I get punished. But that's not the point, is it? What about forgiveness and redemption?"
"Redemption went out with cigarette coupons," said I. "What's on offer?"

"She gets the house and the car," said the Professor. "I get the cottage."
"And the children?" I asked gently.
"They stay with her," said the Professor. "I get equal access. She gets enough money to keep the Child Support Agency off my back."
"Sounds like you get off cheap," said I.
"Bloody expensive as quick fucks go," said the Professor. "I keep wishing I'd left the greenhouse lights off. Buy us another beer, why don't you?"
"Your turn," said I.

I do like the Professor. His attitude to women is just awful. And he's hopeless with money. But he is my best friend.

"How about yourself?" said the Professor, placing the next two pints on the table.
"Still pretty raw," said I.
"How long's it been now?" said the Professor.
"Nearly two years," said I.
"Still no word from her?" said the Professor.
"Nothing," said I.

OK, I woke up one morning and she'd gone. There was no note. No phone message. No email. Nothing. I went frantic. I asked all our friends. I asked all her friends. I asked her work mates. Nobody knew anything. Well, nobody said they knew anything.

Finally, I asked her parents. Her parents sounded so smug as they told me that she wanted nothing more to do with me. I went crazy. I left my job. I went to all the places we used to go to. All the places she used to go to. Nothing. I asked the police to find her. The police sounded so smug as they told me that she didn't want to be found.

I went totally bananas. I sat in the flat. Our flat. And I stared at the telephone, willing it to ring.

Robin rescued me. Robin had introduced us.

"You won't sell up?" said the Professor.
"It's a flat, not a mausoleum," said I. "It's my home. Why should I sell it?"
"Fresh start?" said the Professor. "Less memories? Usual empty platitudes I suppose. Yeah, stay if you're happy there."
"Who said anything about happiness?" said I. "How about a wee dram?"
"Don't mind if I do," said the Professor. "Is her room still empty?"
"You know it is," said I.
"You don't suppose I could stay there for a bit," said the Professor, "until I get things straightened out. Please?"
"As a stop gap," said I. "You've still got the keys. But only 'til you find somewhere more permanent."
"You're a pal!" said the Professor, as I got up and went back to the bar.

I didn't know where she's gone. I really didn't care. I just wished I knew why.

"Anyway," said the Professor, splitting the brace of Grouse, "you should get away from that bloody shop. And the sanctimonious fool that runs it. She exploits you something rotten."
"You know it barely breaks even," said I. "I can hardly ask her for more money."
"Not surprising given how long it takes them to order anything," said the Professor.
"Got any better suggestions?" said I. "I'm buggered if I'm going back to teaching. She's all right. Heart's in the right place."
"In her holiday home in Tuscany," said the Professor. "You know book selling's mostly a rich man's hobby or a poor man's obsession. She may be obsessed but she's not poor. Off she swans every autumn to write her bloody poetry and you slave away subsidising her vanity publishing."

"So how long ago did she kick you out of her bed?" I asked quietly.
"That's not germane," said the Professor. "I've no time for wealthy bleeding hearts."

At closing time, we helped each other up the Vennel steps and staggered across the Meadows.

"When do you want to move in?" said I.
"How about the morn'?" said the Professor. "I can't face another night on my brother's dining room floor."
"Have you got a lot of stuff?" said I.
"Not yet," said the Professor. "Not until we've signed some sort of settlement. Anyway, I can stash most of it in the lab until I decide what to do."
"I'll clear you some drawers," said I. "I hope your cooking's improved."

We parted company at Jawbone Walk. The Professor went east. I crossed Melville Drive and sauntered south up Marchmont Road.

I felt really lousy by the time I got home. Brains full of pavlova, coughing copiously.

The customer was waiting outside my front door.

"I don't want to sound melodramatic," said the customer, "but you've got to be on the Franco-Swiss border in the next 48 hours."
"Come on!" said I. "I don't know you from Adam!"
"Three day cold," said the customer. "Only two days left. Here are the tickets. Walk over the border south west from Geneva to the téléfèrique. In the cafe on top of the mountain you'll meet this women."

He passed me a photograph. Her photograph. I stared at the picture in utter disbelief.

"Greet her as if you've really missed her," said the customer. "A long lingering kiss. Have a quick cup of coffee. And get the hell out. You've a room booked in the Hotel Cornavin."

"I'm not Tintin," said I, beyond bewildered.

"Your cold," said the customer, handing me an envelope. "It's a rhinovirus. With a Dawkins encoding. You picked it up off his hanky. The dead man's. You can read *River out of Eden* on the plane. The kiss will pass it on to the next stage. If the chain's broken we're all done for."

"I thought chain letters were illegal," said I, brains jangling.

The van screeched to a halt. Strong arms forced me back against the wall.

"The epiphany machine!" screamed the customer as they wrestled him into the back of the van. "You must…"

"Special Branch," said the arms. "You don't want trouble. Best forget this ever happened, eh?"

Numb from the neck up, I went into the flat and scrutinised the photo. She looked much the same. That's not true. She looked happy.

I checked the envelope. Plane tickets. A direct Edinburgh to Geneva return flight. Next morning. In my name. I looked in the desk and dug out my passport. The European visa still had a month to run and was good for a week at a time.

Snuffling, I took a couple of paracetemol and lay down on the sofa.

When I woke up I wished I hadn't. Several cups of weak Earl Gray later, I phoned Robin. She sounded somewhat peeved and didn't offer to take me to the airport. I didn't ask.

Only away for a couple of days. Lots of space in the backpack for pants, socks, a book or two and the spare glasses.

I left the Professor a note on the kitchen table, watered the plants and locked all the windows. As an afterthought I left a new message on the answer phone. Usually I compose them carefully and play ear catching music in the background. Your answer phone says so much about you: make that first impression count, with a quote from the Trappists or a burst of Cage. No time for such niceties, alas. "Pay a ten pound fine or take a chance, after the tone."

I dropped by the shop for a copy of *River out of Eden*. Robin was unpacking the replacement machine. I offered to help but she waved me away.

"Have a good trip," she said gamely. "I'll put the book on your account."
"Thanks," said I. "Do you want anything from Geneva?"
"Actually," said Robin "a friend of mine runs a really good second hand bookshop above the Reformation Monument in the old town. Last time I saw him he said he'd look out for anything in English he thought might interest me. The shop's called *Le Cerveau Affame* and he's called Felix, like the cat. I'll write it all down."
"Does he know what you like?" said I.
"Oh yes," said Robin. "Just take anything he offers and I'll sort out the payment from this end."
"Right," said I. "I'll look him up. See you the morn'."
"Monday's fine," said Robin. "You must be due some holiday."
"I'll send you a postcard," said I.

I put the details in my pocket and bade Robin farewell. Up George IV Bridge and over the Mound, thronged with tourists escaping from endless Royal Mile shops full of Taiwanese tartanry, down the side of the Gardens to the tram stop opposite Waverly Station.

The tram was packed. I stood all the way.

After checking in I queued for security. My whole body X-ray exposure for the past six months was way over the safety limits so they made do with a strip search. Impersonal. Occasionally painful. Uniformly undignified.

I walked through the duty free mall, bought a paper at the newsagent's and joined the next queue for the tube to the aircraft.

Most flying's about as exotic as being trapped on a long distance bus with no service station stops. This plane was filthy and they'd put in an extra row of seats. At least they'd dispensed with the safety warnings: there aren't too many instances of successful sea evacuations after hitting the water from 30,000 feet.

After take off I realised that I'd no change for the food dispenser and I'd seen the film twice before. Mercifully, I was by the window in the exit aisle with no one next to me. I dug out the Dawkins, folded up the arm rest, stretched my legs diagonally across the row and began to browse:

> *"...From there it would be short work to read the full English text of Professor Crickson's message, sneezed around the world..."*

2. On the border

After the indignities of departure, arrival was easy. I sauntered off the 'plane, across the concourse, and onto a waiting train for the ten minute journey into central Geneva. The Hotel Cornavin was just as I'd remembered it. Brown. Discreet. Expensive. Tatty. Someone had stuck a Gay Pride sticker on the plaster model of Herge's hero in the foyer: Snowy sported a lecherous grin.

But the concièrge was expecting me and I was swiftly installed en-suite with a view across the source of the Rhone to the city centre on the heights above. I called room service and showered to pass the time: I wasn't in any hurry. That's not true. I was in a hurry but not in any rush.

After a gentle lunch I walked down the pedestrian precinct at the back of the station, past the Post Office and rows of shops selling army knives and cuckoo clocks. When it comes to tourism, the Swiss have no scruples about stereotypes. Over the bridge where the lake becomes the river and through the Jardin Anglaise, dodging dope dealers. I'm not averse to the occasional toke but I'd another border to negotiate.

Really! How long can I keep this derivative hard-boiled nonsense up for?

The tram to the French border took half an hour. Before we left the EU, crossing was a formality, as indeed it still is for the Swiss. But today a British passport is an invitation to a dingy shed and another set of cold, rubber fingers in the orifices.

It was mid-afternoon when I finally arrived at the bottom station for the Mont Saleve téléfèrique. The mountain itself isn't particularly imposing though still steep enough for suicides and hang gliders.

Just beyond the top station was the cafe. She was sitting at an outside table.

"I knew you'd come when you saw the photo," she said.
"Napier's bones?" said I.
"Later," she said, looking round hurriedly. "Give us a kiss then."
"Anything to oblige," said I, pecking her on the cheek.
"Not like that," she said, pulling my head down and rapidly exploring the inside of my mouth with her tongue.
"Was it good for you?" I said, sitting down opposite her.
"Don't be like that!" she said. "Coffee?"
"Weak Earl Grey with a slice of lemon," said I.
"Come on!" she said, "This is France!" and ordered a cappuccino from the lurking waiter.

"So how long's it been?" she said.
"Nearly two years," said I. "You know that fine."
"Counted every last second have you?" she said.
"Indeed I have," said I.

The waiter brought the coffee. I emptied a sachet of brown sugar into the speckled froth and stirred listlessly.

"Why did you leave?" I said finally.
"Why did you stay?" she said.
"It was my flat," said I.
"It was my home!" said she.
"No note, no explanation, nothing," said I.

"I told Robin," she said.

"Oh yes?" said I. "What did you tell Robin?"

"Didn't she tell you?" she said.

"She said you'd left," said I, "and that I shouldn't blame myself, or something equally anodyne. What did you tell her?"

"Not here," she said. "I've a room in Annemasse. How are you off for time?"

"I've all the time in the world," said I. "I only came to see you. But the person who told me to come also told me to get the hell out as soon as I could."

"Nonsense!" she said. "You're perfectly safe. Well, here in France anyway. Drink up."

The 2CV was in the lot next to the cafe.

"Have you still got keys?" she said.

"It was our car," said I.

"It's my car," she said. "Do you want to drive?"

"You drive," said I.

Round the mountain and onto the highway. It's always disconcerting being in the front passenger seat on the wrong side of the road. The EU's attempt to make the UK change over was the last straw for the little Englanders, especially so soon after the mile was finally abolished.

"So what have you been doing here?" said I.

"Who said I'd been here?" she said.

"Well, you are here, aren't you?" said I.

"Indeed I am," she said, "but that doesn't mean I'm doing anything here other than being here."

"This is all a bit gnomic," said I.

"Indeed it is," she said.

Off at the second exit.

"Did you remember the one about the Frenchman who asked for pastis in Penzance?" said I.
"I told it to you," she said.
"I know," said I.

The room was in a flat in a nondescript modern block. Lift. Concierge. Entry phone. Basement parking.

She took off her coat.

"I'm going to have a shower," she said, casually. "Would you care to join me?"

Nobody knows how to teach computer programming. I've tried language immersion, structured design, top-down decomposition, modulation, object orientation. It makes no difference: either they learn or they don't.

Nobody knows how to write about sex either. Male view. Female view. Birds-eye view. Anatomical neo-realism. Lyrical similes. Humorous blunderings. No one can capture in words just how it feels. Maybe sex is the ultimate qualia, the proof of phenomenological doubt. How can you know what it's like to experience someone else's sexuality when you can't even externalise something you know as well as your own orgasm?

I didn't crash the yoghurt cart. She made all the right noises. So did I. We fell asleep in a heap in each other's arms in the warm late afternoon sunlight.

When I woke up, she was sitting in the armchair watching me, fully dressed.

"You better go," she said.
"Napier's bones?" said I.
"You got what you came for," she said.

"No I didn't," said I.

"Get your kit on," she said. "There's a bus back to Geneva every thirty minutes from the main square."

"But I don't understand!" said I.

"What's to understand?" said she.

"Why are you doing this to me?" said I.

"Doing what?" said she.

The customer stepped into the room.

"Need a hand?" he said.

"No," said I. "No. No."

Rejected. Despised. A man of sorrow.

I climbed into my clothes. They both watched, saying nothing.

"No explanations at all?" said I, tying the other shoe lace.

"None," she said.

"Bastards!" said I. "Why me?"

"Oh come on," said the customer. "Isn't it obvious? Who else would've come halfway across Europe for a kiss? Anyway, we should thank you for being so predictable."

"This is mad!" said I. "This time yesterday you were being kidnapped by Special Branch!"

They both laughed.

"Special Branch?" said the customer. "Says who? Anyway, are you sure it was me you saw?"

"Of course it was you!" said I.

"Of course it was," said the customer.

"Coat on," she said. "What are you waiting for? Off you go. Don't forget to leave the car keys."

"But I don't know what to do!" said I.

"You could tell us to stop treating you like a child," she said. "You could hurl yourself at one of us, pinion them to the ground and beat the shit out of them. You could calmly pick up the phone and call the police. You could smash up the flat in a manic frenzy. You could tell us to be reasonable and demand to discuss things rationally. You could burst into tears and beg me to come back to you. You could leave quietly, with dignity. You could coldly and deliberately break something of value. You could insist that my colleague leave so we can sort out unfinished personal business. You could whimper in a corner. It's all the same to me. What do you fancy?"

Neither of them offered me a lift. I didn't ask.

In a daze, I walked through the streets to the express bus stop. The journey was quick and the Swiss border guard was cursory.

No duty free on buses. Back in the hotel, room service obliged with an astonishingly expensive bottle of Scotch.

Fortified by my native tincture, did I hail a taxi in a half-cut fury? Did I sit on the back seat, seething, as I crossed the fourth wall? Did I stand outside the flat, watching their shadows on the window blind above? Did I hammer furiously on the door, only stopping when a neighbour told me that the flat had been empty for months? Did I descend the basement steps as the 2CV roared off up the ramp? None of the above.

A steady stream of drams soon stilled the jumping beans in the brain. Systems analysis. Napier's bones. A conspiracy? But communism is the happy philosophy and the class struggle is the engineer of human souls, not men called Thursday with black capes and bombs labelled 'bomb'.

I left the hotel and wandered the streets. Back on the pedestrian precinct I entered a dim and smoky coffee bar. Cool jazz poured from the jukebox. The waiters wore black jeans and polo necks. Almost all the tables were full of Alexandrian quartets, jabbering away earnestly.

The table by the toilets sported the largest man I'd ever seen, ripples of fat emerging from neck and cuffs.

"Is this seat taken?" said I, gesturing towards the obviously unoccupied Bauhaus chair.
"Be my guest," said the London accent. "Where do you hail from?"
"I'm from the end of history," said I.
"I'm from the end of time," said the man. "And I don't think much of these temporal co-ordinates."
"Dr Who?" said I. "Or H.G.Wells? Or Jerek Karnelian?"
"Lost in the myths of time," said the man. "You better order. The service here's lousy."

The menu was the predictable post-modern mix of focaccia bread and lemon grass. But then all food is bricolage unless you live on a desert island.

I flagged down a waiter. Soup of the day was rocket and sorrel with white pumpernickel.

"What are you drinking?" asked the man. "The Jura wine is excellent."
"White please," said I, "grape and grain notwithstanding."
"A fellow whiskeyphile," said the man, "or my name's not Haddock."
"Come on!" said I. "Captain Haddock is Scots."
"Captain Haddock is scotch," said the man, "judging by how much he drank, if you subscribe to the third policeman's molecular theory of course."
"Ripped off from Tristram Shandy's uncle," said I.
"And my name really is Haddock," said the man. "Felix Haddock."

The soup arrived. It was tepid and tasteless, and the bread was made of recycled computer cards, but I was suddenly very hungry.

The wine was cold and fruity dry.

"The bookseller?" said I, mouth full.
"My fame clearly precedes me," said Felix. "And whose company do I currently have the pleasure of?"
"Didn't Robin phone you from Edinburgh?" said I.
"Aha!" said Felix. "The wanderlusty employee! What a coincidence!"

Coincidences don't happen. Not that things are meant to happen but there's always a good reason.

"Of course my flat is two floors up, and I've had supper here every night for five years," said Felix. "What brought you?"
"Hunger and horror," said I.

I finished the soup and reconsulted the menu. The main courses sounded disgusting. Olive oil and balsamic vinegar dripped from the descriptions. Another waiter floated by, avoiding eye contact. Felix stuck out an arm, bringing him up short.

I ordered in broken French. Frankly I had no idea what I would end up with. And cared less.

"Oh, you'll enjoy that!" said Felix. "How daring. Most Brits don't have the first idea about food."
"What have I asked for?" said I.
"You'll see," said Felix. "More wine?" making a long arm.

"How do you know Robin?" said I.

"Everyone knows Robin," said Felix. "Everywhere I've been I've met people who know Robin."

"You exaggerate, surely?" said I.

"I do not," said Felix. "Or my name's not Ian."

"I thought you were called Felix," said I.

"Felix Ian," said Felix. "Second hand bookselling circles aren't so big."

"We don't sell second hand books," said I. "Well, not so you'd notice. One small shelf of rubbish brought in by penniless supplicants. We give them twenty-five percent of the cover price and sell them for fifty percent."

"Nice mark-up," said Felix. "I bet no one buys them."

The smoked eels and pumpkin in Emmental and marsala sauce made me regret bunking off all those conversational French classes. The rest of the wine helped. I ordered another bottle.

"How can you possibly afford to live here?" said I. "There's no money in books."

"Maybe not in the UK," said Felix. "But Geneva's awash with first editions in any language you choose."

"So you ship them over to Robin?" said I.

"Certainly do," said Felix. "She sends back feminist detective stories. The expats and native intellectuals gobble them up. English language books are really expensive here."

"But we don't sell first editions," said I.

"You don't but Robin does," said Felix. "How do you think she can afford to holiday in Italy?"

"I always assumed she had a private income," said I. "Never asked."

"No," said Felix. "It's not polite in progressive circles is it?"

Replete, I pushed the plate away. The sauce had long congealed on the pumpkin rind. I tooth-picked fragments of eel from between the teeth while Felix negotiated coffee.

"I really fancy a cigarette," said Felix, reaching in his pocket and pulling out a pack of Black Russians. "Would you like one?"

"That's the brand that Boris smokes," said I, taking one.

"You're staying at the Cornavin, aren't you" said Felix.

"How did you guess," said I.

"Where else would a fellow member of the Society for Sober Sailors stay?" said Felix.

"You don't sound Scots," said I.

"Moved south when I was three," said Felix. "But I'm Scots or my name's not Stuart."

"Get away," said I, topping up the glasses. "Felix Ian Stuart Haddock?"

"What's that spell?" said Felix.

The coffee arrived. A sorrowful wedge of lemon attempted to escape from the peat brown tea.

"Cryptic clue?" said I.

"Mother was a fiend for the Scotsman crossword," said Felix.

"If you had a son would you call him Francis?" said I.

"Naturally!" said Felix.

I rescued the lemon, and sipped cautiously.

"Fancy a liqueur?" said Felix.

"What goes with tea?" said I. "Do they sell sympathy? I'm three-quarters cut already."

Felix waved at a trawling waiter and two globes of Armagnac appeared as if by pneumatic tube.

He stared at me pensively.

"Well, aren't you going to ask me?" he said finally.

"Maybe I'm too polite," said I. "What am I supposed to ask you?"

"Why I'm so blubbery," said Felix. "Nothing wrong with the glands. Straight gluttony."

No. Don't say it.

"Frankly," said I, "it's not very attractive."

"Why do you think I want to attract you?" said Felix.

"That's not what I meant," said I, hastily.

"Why on earth not?" said Felix. "Don't you fancy a quick wank?"

"Goodness!" said I. "We've barely met. And I've never done it with anyone else."

"Nor have I," said Felix, "but there's no time like the present. Anyway, you're now so guilty about suggesting that I'm not attractive that you can hardly refuse."

"Do you always talk to strangers like this?" said I.

"You're not strange," said Felix. "Anyway, isn't this how men are supposed to talk? Bonding?"

"Aha!" said I. "A men's group man. They're such fucking hypocrites. Half of them do it so they can sleep with heterosexual feminists. The other half don't care which women they sleep with if only they could work out how to ask them without being rejected. What's in it for you?"

"Look..." said Felix.

"Spare me your lectures about patriarchy," said I. "Right now I really don't give a toss."

"What a pity," said Felix. "You might learn something."

"I need to explore the bisexuality within me, do I?" said I.

"What you need," said Felix, "is your own fresh sperm, warm on your belly. Though I doubt if you could get it up."

"You sure know how to hurt a boy," said I, getting up.

"Could we start again please?" said Felix. "I was enjoying it to begin with. Have another brandy?"

"Is this seat taken?" said I, gesturing towards my obviously unoccupied Bauhaus chair.

"Be my guest," said the London accent. "Where do you hail from?"

Two evenings solid drinking. It would be false induction to presume that this is my primary pastime. Napier's bones. If not a conspiracy then what? I was tired and emotional and needed to attain the horizontal.

"I really must be off," said I. "What time do you open?"

"I'll be open when you get there," said Felix. "Are you sure you won't come out to play?"

"I think not," said I. "We'd better get the bill."

"I'll pay," said Felix. "It's the least I can do."

Back at the hotel, the night porter handed me an envelope with the key. He'd no idea who'd left it. I took the lift up to my room, shed clothing for the second time that day and lay down.

The next thing I knew it was broad daylight and the phone was ringing. My room was only paid for until mid day and it was already eleven a.m. Did I want to extend my stay? I did not. I asked for a substantial fried breakfast and began to dress.

The envelope fell out of my underpants. The note said "Leave now." Anything to oblige. I found the fresh pair in the bag and dressed hurriedly.

Sausage, egg, bacon, steak, beans, tomatoes, fried potato. None of your namby pamby continental crispbread and yoghurt nonsense. No black pudding or haggis, alas, but the dripping smelt fresh and the butter was salted. A large pot of tea chased toast and honey.

I felt surprisingly good. Considering nothing.

I returned the keys to the concierge and headed south once more, this time to the old town, high above the lake. *Le Cerveau Affame* was in a row of tall, austere, grey shops, on a terrace, looking out across the road above the vast graven images of Protestant fundamentalism.

The sign in the window read "Back in 5 minutes". I tried the door handle. Unlocked. Of course I went in.

By the front door the usual accoutrements of the book trade: computer; CD ROMs of 'Books in Print' and publishers catalogues; a phone; a credit card reader. Beyond, a chasm of twilight shelves.

I stepped forward and looked around. There was no sign of any other browsers. I inspected the shelves, each neatly labelled. The classification was the usual alphabetical by topic and author, but carefully sectioned by publication date into blocks of 10 years. Nearest the door, last year's best sellers. Deeper in, paperbacks slowly gave way to livre de poche, leather displaced pasteboard. Intrigued, I traced the decades back to nineteen hundred and found myself at the rear of the shop at the top of a spiral staircase. An arrow marked "Nineteenth Century" beckoned downwards.

The basement was deeper than the first floor, extending forwards under the road. Nearest the stairs was a long table with a selection of pristine fin de siècle art publications. All first editions. Once again, two tall rows of shelves stretched away into the gloom. Back at the front of the shop was another spiral staircase with another descending arrow: "Eighteenth Century". All around, above and below, words oozed from the endless pages, calling, imploring, demanding to be read.

I heard a noise above and ascended to modernity.

"Aha!" said Felix. "I wondered when you'd show up. Somewhat the worse for wear I'll bet."

"Never felt better," said I. "How's yourself?"

"Just fine, thank you," said Felix. "What a very English conversation. Maybe we should shake hands?"

"The endless search for bodily contact?" said I.

"Ah my beauty past compare," said Felix. "What do you make of the shop?"

"Trusting of you to leave the door open," said I.

"I knew you were coming," said Felix. "What do you think of the stock?"

"I'm puzzled by your layout," said I. "How do you ever find anything?"

"I know the shelves backwards," said Felix. "Anyway, it's all on the computer."

"But why divide things up chronologically?" said I. "It must make browsing really frustrating."

"Well," said Felix, "most recent second hand stock is complete rubbish but if you keep anything long enough it acquires historical or rarity value. Most of my customers are collectors, not readers and they know what they're after by date and topic."

"You don't seem to have many customers," said I looking round.

"I mostly sell through mail order," said Felix. "I send out specialist catalogues which are advertised in collector's magazines."

"You've got an amazing range," said I. "Do you really have a entire floor of eighteenth century stuff?"

Felix laughed. "You haven't seen the half of it," he said. "There's been a bookshop on this site for over 300 years. Every time it changed hands the stock went with it."

"But it must be worth a fortune!" said I. "How could you afford to buy it?"

"Who said I bought it?" said Felix. "Anyway, that's why it's all chronological. Each new owner steadily pushed the older stuff to the back. I just systematised it all."

"How do you know what to keep?" said I.

"Well," said Felix, "only three sorts of books survive. Take the perennial hardys, your bog standard classics, your dead Caucasians. They stay in circulation 'til the spines give way so they're always a safe bet. It's really good if you can spot someone recent who ends up joining the canon."

"That makes sense," said I.

"Then you get massive best sellers," said Felix, "like the ones sold in airport lounges and railway station newsagents. They get thrown out when they lose topicality but there's enough of them around for a few to survive in jumble sales. Then you suddenly get fads for particular periods or authors, and they start to sell again. I'll give you an example. When I took over here, there was a shelf of worthless hardbacks by nineteen twenties women, left behind by inter-war holiday makers and health cure fanatics. But when feminism generated an interest in lost women writers in the late seventies, their books were all out of copyright so publishers like Virago were able to reissue them to subsidise new authors. As a side effect, the originals' prices shot up more or less overnight."

"You said three sorts of books survived?" said I.

"The total flops have a curious persistence," said Felix. "They mostly get pulped but quite often they're dumped at rock bottom prices as remainders. The trick's to buy them up and junk ninety percent of them."

"Aren't you taking a bit of a gamble?" said I. "Murphy swore by low profit and high turnover."

"Solipsist's choice," said Felix. "If you keep absolutely any book for long enough it'll sell to someone who wants to own it rather than read it. Does it matter if people queued to buy it when it first appeared or if it was published by an embittered crank with private means? I've got three floors of books that were probably abject turkeys in their days. I can live quite comfortably if I can sell one eighteenth century volume a week."

"You said there'd been a shop here for over three hundred years," said I. "You must have older books than that."

"Must I? said Felix, quickly. "How about a bite to eat?"

"I thought you had something for Robin," said I.

"Oh yes," said Felix, reaching behind the front desk and pulling out a brown paper parcel. "Could you give this to her? The price's inside."

"Is that all?" said I, putting the parcel into my bag. "I'd expected more."

"Robin's got very distinctive tastes," said Felix. "I'm sure she'll be pleased with it. Anyway, when's your flight?"

I checked the tickets.

"Two p.m.," said I.

"Loads of time," said Felix. "Let's eat and then I'll drive you to the airport."

"What about the shop?" said I.

"Oh, I sold a book this morning!" said Felix. "That'll do for today."

"Won't I need to declare it or fill in customs forms or something?" said I.

"Nothing like that," said Felix. "They'll just x-ray it and wave you through."

Napier's bones. How did I know it was a book, not paedophile photographs or a kilo of crack cocaine? Felix was an abject pillock but I trusted Robin.

Felix shut up the shop. We walked through the old town towards the lake.

"You're very quiet," said Felix, as we started down the steps at the side of the cathedral.

"How about this one?" said I, stopping and peering into a cafe window.

"What's the difference between a safety restraint and Alexander Trochi?" said Felix, as the waitress showed us to a table.

"No clues," said I, sitting down.

"One's a seat belt and the other's a Beat Celt," said Felix, accepting a menu.

"That's awful," said I.

"What's the difference between the Trustee Savings Bank and Sir Walter Raleigh?" said Felix, passing the menu to me.

"Haven't the faintest," said I. "Ham and cheese croissant, and a weak tea with lemon, please."

"One's the bank that likes to say 'Yes'", said Felix, "and the other's the Yank that likes to say 'Bess'."

"Sir Walter Raleigh wasn't really American," said I.

"Poetic license," said Felix. "Don't be so pedantic. I'll have a strawberry pancake and ice cream to start with. Will you join me in a schnapps?"

"Not for me," said I.

"What's the difference between a kookaburra and the film 'The Road to Kabul'?" said Felix.

"I shudder to think," said I.

"One's king of the bush," said Felix, "and the other's Bing of the Kush."

"Sorry?" said I.

"Bing Crosby?" said Felix. "'The Road to Kabul'?"

"How slow of me," said I. "Do you make them up?"

"Endlessly," said Felix. "Do I detect a note of irritation?"

"Surely not," said I.

The food arrived. We ate in silence. Not an awkward silence. Not a pregnant silence. Not a silence broken only by the ticking of a clock or the rattle of hail on the window. Just silence.

"What next?" said Felix.

"That's enough for me," said I. "I'll get some apology for lunch on the flight."

"I won't," said Felix. "A steak Bernaise shouldn't take long."

"You still eat beef?" said I.

"Of course," said Felix. "Someone's got to."

"If you say so," said I.

Felix walked over to the cash desk. I picked up the book of matches from the ashtray and fiddled with it. Felix came back with a large bottle of mineral water.

"You don't like me much, do you?" said Felix.

"Why on earth do you say that?" said I. "I hardly know you."

"I'm large and loud and forward," said Felix. "Whereas you're quiet and superior."

"Am I supposed to apologise for not fancying you?" said I.

"How about a gesture of reconciliation?" said Felix.

"I came to the shop, didn't I," said I.

"You're an addict," said Felix. "You can't keep away from books. Otherwise, why on earth would you go on working for Robin?"

"Napier's bones," said I.

"No, it's a fillet," said Felix, as the steak arrived.

"I'm awa to powder my nose," said I, putting the matches into my coat pocket.

When I returned from the small but perfectly formed toilet, the customer was sitting in my chair.

"Friend of yours?" said Felix, mouth full.

"What the fuck are you doing here?" said I.

"Didn't you get my note?" said the customer. "If you're not on that flight there'll be hell to pay."

"There'll be hell to pay if I don't get some sense out of someone," said I.

"You really are very stubborn," said the customer. "Why don't you just come with me and we can straighten things out."

"Not a chance," said I.

"You're making a big mistake," said the customer.

"It's you that's making the mistake," said Felix, getting up and sitting on him.

"Off you go," he said to me. "Don't forget your bag."

"Thanks," said I.

"Fidgee fidgee," said Felix.

"Boodle boodle," said I.

I ran down the hill and hailed a taxi on the main street. The journey to the airport was uneventful if expensive.

In the lounge, I checked in and headed off to international departures. The parcel went straight through the scanner, no questions asked. At the control desk I handed over my passport.

"This is no use," said the frontier guard.
"What do you mean?" said I.
"It's registered in Glasgow," said the frontier guard.
"So what?" said I. "It's a current British passport, it got me in here all right. Twice."
"There must have been a mistake," said the frontier guard. "Our government doesn't recognise them anymore if they're issued in Scotland."
"Don't be daft, man," said I.
"Do you have a Scottish passport?" said the frontier guard.
"What on earth for?" said I. "I don't need one. Technically I'm a dual national."
"I'm afraid there's nothing more I can do for you," said the frontier guard. "Would you accompany these gentlemen, please."

Two suits emerged from a side door.

"This way, please," said one.
"What's going on?" said I.
"It appears that you're stateless," said the other. "Come with us, please."
"Where are you taking me?" said I.
"To the resettlement centre," said one. "Please don't argue. We really don't want a scene."

3. In the cell

The resettlement centre was on the outskirts of Yverdon les Bains, a fading spa town to the north-east of Geneva. At first sight, it seemed most unlike the desolate disused airfields used in England to isolate and humiliate asylum seekers. The central stone building was framed on three sides by long, low, white, breeze block huts, divided internally into single and group rooms. On the fourth side was a small indoor heated swimming pool, presumably fed from the same source as the spa.

We arrived in the late afternoon and I was delivered up to the reception office. I explained my circumstances to the immigration officer and asked to see the British Consul. She laughed and told me that the Consulate reopened at ten a.m. on Monday. I then asked to see the Scottish Consul. She consulted a large file and made a phone call. The Scottish Consul would see me next morning. In the meantime, I was to avail myself of their hospitality. I was free to go where ever I liked within the camp but under no circumstances would I be allowed to leave without a recognised passport. Had I considered applying for Swiss nationality? I had not. I was given a pocket camp directory and a temporary refugee ID card which I was to show it if I needed any services.

I was taken next to the stores. I declined the offer of a complete set of slightly used clothing, pointing out that I hoped to be reunited with my own sartorial selection in the very near future. Instead, I asked for a pair of swimming trunks. Clutching a towel and a bag of toilet requisites, I was shown around the rest of the main building - dining hall, shop, medical centre, non-denominational meeting place, library - and then escorted to the hut opposite the front steps.

My room was three metres square, with an iron bed, a small chest of drawers, a chair and a central heating radiator. The window was barred and opened inwards. The door locked from the outside only and had a peephole.

Was I angry? Upset? Frightened? Belligerent? Worried? Napier's bones. Far worse things might happen.

I dumped my things on the bed and ambled down the corridor to the day room. A small group was huddled round the TV, morosely watching cricket on the BSkyB World Service. I sat down in a vacant chair.

"Been here long?" said I, to no one in particular.
"A couple of weeks," said the older woman in a broad Ulster accent. "We're from East Belfast. We thought that we'd find our own kind here after you bastards abandoned us."
"I'm from Edinburgh," said I.
"You don't talk Scots," said the woman.
"I'm not Scots," said I.
"Well fuck off then," said the woman.
"If I'm English, why am I here?" said I.
"Give the lad a break," said the older man.
"Can you tell me a couple of things about this place, please?" said I.
"What's to tell?" said the woman.
"Can I phone or send letters?" said I.
"Have you got any money?" said the woman. "You can do what you like if you've got money. This is Switzerland."
"Does the shop sell stamps?" said I.

"It does," said the woman, "but you'd better hurry."

I returned to my room, retrieved the parcel, towel, trunks and toiletries and made my way to the shop. I addressed the parcel to myself, marked it as urgent and handed it over for courier delivery. I then circled the courtyard, in search of the pool entrance.

The attendant in the foyer looked up briefly from their magazine and waved me in. Up the stairs and through the glass doors. The pool was white tiled, twenty-five metres long and ten metres wide, with lanes marked in blue. On either side a row of cubicles. The high angular translucent roof was supported with blue wooden beams.

The pool was empty; the water flat and crystal clear.

I went into number thirteen, for luck, undressed and put on the trunks. New swimming costumes always feel odd. Unfamiliar bands round waist and groin. Draw string, not elastic sided. Green.

Beyond the deep end, I entered the shower room and pushed the first button. The rosette sprayed ice cold; tension head pain as it hit my feet. I tried each of the other three in turn. Adequately wet, I returned to the pool, took a deep breath and dived in, clumsily. Blood temperature water engulfed me. Left arm, right arm, breathe, kicking. Near the shallow end my fingers grazed the bottom. I pushed off on my back and kicked leisurely up to the deep end, arms by my side. Through the roof the light was fading. At the deep end, I pushed off again on my front: left arm, right arm, breathe, kicking. Twenty lengths is five hundred metres, in twenty minutes is one and a half kilometres per hour. About a quarter the speed of walking.

I learned to swim many years ago in the Lime Grove Baths in Hammersmith, near the BBC studios. Every Wednesday, one of my parents would take me to the Water Gypsies for lessons. Afterwards we'd buy a fish supper from a nearby chip shop, wrapped in old TV scripts. Once my mum found an entire Hancock episode. I wonder if the pool's still there? I used to really like swimming but got out of the way of it when I left home. These days I try to go to the local pool once or twice at the weekend. I'm not a strong swimmer but it helps maintain what passes for fitness.

On length eighteen, a striking woman, mid thirties's, blue one piece costume, trundled herself to the pool side in her wheelchair and slipped into the water. No legs past the knees. She launched off, her sinuous, muscular arms lending speed and grace I could only envy.

I completed the last two lengths and hauled myself along the pool rim to the steps. Back to the cubicle for soap and shampoo. Back to the showers. Shampoo the beard and what remains of the hair, and wash all over. In the cubicle, off with the trunks and towel down from head to feet. Clothes on: pants, T shirt, shirt, socks, jeans; jersey; coat. Swiss roll the trunks in the folded towel. As I left the pool area, the woman traversed its length without pause.

In my block the Orangepersons were still watching television. The older woman looked up.

"There's been a phone call for you," said she.
"Any message?" said I.
"None," said she. "Sounded a bit like you though."
"Thanks," said I.

Who sounds like me? Apart from me. Not the customer. Felix maybe, on a bad line?

I hung the towel and trunks over the radiator in my cell and returned once more to the main building. The canteen was empty, the service self, the food more school dinner than oat cuisine: tepid, over-cooked and plentiful. I ladled potatoes, cabbage and what looked like mutton stew onto a plate and sat down at a table by a window looking out across a valley to mountains. The stew tasted excellent: the broth a piquant blend of tomato and paprika.

Since leaving the airport my brain had been write only. Too much to take in. Too much to piece together. Not enough glue. Food helps. Why Napier's bones? All I knew was that they were an early system for doing multiplication and division, by manipulating rods with the times tables on them, a sort of slide rule precursor, not that anyone remembers what a slide rule is anymore unless they read Neville Shute novels. The oldest surviving university in Edinburgh is named after him, his ancestral tower the focal point of a vast city centre campus.

As I scraped the plate clean with a spoon, the woman from the pool came into the canteen.

"Would you help me please?" she said.

Why do foreigners always communicate effortlessly in faultless English? Well they don't, but negotiating dialect is tiresome. As are misunderstandings based on metalinguistic confusion. Why bother? We want semantics, not phonemes.

"Of course," said I, standing up. "What would you like?".
"Whatever you had," said she. "It's all much the same."
"Have you been here long?" said I, doling out another plateful.
"Four days," said she. "They've only just let me out of hospital."
"Where are you from?" said I, carrying the plate over to my table.
"Afghanistan," said she. "Could we go over there, please. That table's a bit lower."

"Sorry," said I.

"Don't apologise," she said. "Ever since my legs were blown off nobody's stopped apologising. Anyway, where are you from?"

"Scotland," said I.

"So what are you doing here?" said she.

"I was going to have a cup of tea," said I. "Might I join you?"

"Of course," said she. "Could you get me some as well, please, with lots of sugar. The water's foul, just like in Moscow."

I went back to the service shelf, put two tea bags into a large white teapot, filled it with boiling water from the urn, placed it on a tray with two cups, two saucers, a bowl of sugar and a teaspoon, and rejoined the charioteer.

"What were you doing in Moscow?" said I, putting the tray on the table and sitting down.

"Studying Russian and English," said she, pouring the tea. "Sugar?"

"No thanks," said I. "Are you trying to get back to Russia?"

"Like hell I am," said she. "They sold us down the river just like you western liberals. Anyway, you never answered my question."

Repetition becomes tiresome.

"... so it's really a bureaucratic mix up," I finished, laconically. "I should be out of here the morn. How did you wind up here?"

"We got out of Kandahar on foot when the Taliban returned," she said. "We were trying to cross the mountains into Pakistan. Our guide led us into a mine field. The next thing I knew I was lying in a hospital bed in Peshawar. They told me that I was picked up by a relief column. The rest of my family are dead."

I said nothing.

"Don't look so glum," said she. "I'm happy to be alive. I weep for those left behind, not for myself."

"Do you want to stay in Switzerland?" said I.

"I'd really like to go to Vietnam or Angola," she said, "but they've got enough cripples already so I'm trying to get into Australia. There's a story in our family that my father's great uncle went out there as a camel driver before they built the railways. The Australian authorities are searching for relatives for me. I hope his family kept his name."

"What did you make of Moscow?" said I.

"It was amazing!" said she. "Imagine a city where there's always food and running water and electricity and street lighting and winter heating. Where no one abuses you just because you're a woman."

"What about all the corruption?" said I.

"All societies are corrupt," said she. "Why should they be any different? Once they had a ruling principle with the promise of change for the better for everyone. Once they actually tried to put their money where their mouths were. How many universities does Scotland run just for Third World people? And they've thrown it all away. Look at them now, they've got a South American not a Scandinavian economy. They've got the Mafia not a welfare state. They were far far better off before, warts and all."

"Socialism or barbarism?" said I, lamely.

"Tell me about it," said she.

I felt sad and empty. Displacement activity. I stood up and tidied off the table onto the tray.

"Do you want anything else?" said I.

"No thanks," said she. "I need to get some sleep. I've a limb fitting first thing tomorrow."

"Do you want a hand home?" said I.

"You could give me a push," she said. "My arms really ache after the swimming."

"Which block are you in?" said I, as we left the main building.

"Round to the right," she said.

I shoved her wheelchair up the ramp and into her hut.

"I won't ask you in," she said. "We haven't been introduced."

"Right," said I. "Hang on though and I'll give you my details. Should you wind up in Scotland, do get in touch."

"That's unlikely," said she, as I wrote my name, address and phone number on the back of a book shop card, "but thanks anyway. I hope you can do something about whatever it is that's upsetting you so much."

"Is that obvious?" said I, handing her the card.

"Sleep well," said she, trundling down the corridor.

I was wide awake and restless so I thought I'd try the library. A small room, reminiscent of the multi-lingual book exchanges in holiday resorts. If you're cooped up you learn to value books. Perhaps as each refugee became a citizen, they'd left their packets of words for those that would follow. The English language section was a curious rag bag: complete runs of Charles Dickens and Walter Scott, probably thrown out in an Embassy spring cleaning, flanked by soft back shop-and-fuck. No reference books.

An ageing PC stood on a table in one corner. I turned it on. Windows 05. Hopelessly dated. Networking software but no connection to anywhere. I flicked through the stack of CD ROMs. Amongst the games, Microsoft's Encarta encyclopaedia. The world as sound bite. I stuck it in the drive and clicked it awake:

Epiphany (Greek epiphaneia, "appearance"), feast celebrated on January 6 by the Anglican, Eastern, and Roman Catholic churches. The feast originated, and is still recognized in the Eastern Church, as the anniversary of the baptism of Christ. In the Western churches, Epiphany commemorates principally the revelation to the Gentiles of Jesus Christ as the Savior, as portrayed by the coming of the Three Wise Men (see Matthew 2:1-12). In both the Eastern and Western churches the feast secondarily commemorates the marriage at Cana (see John 2:1-11), at which Christ performed his first miracle. Epiphany, known to have been observed earlier than AD 194, is older than Christmas and has always been a festival of the highest rank. The eve of Epiphany is called Twelfth Night, and the day itself is sometimes referred to as Twelfth Day. In England, the sovereign commemorates the day by offering gold, frankincense, and myrrh at the altar in the Chapel Royal, at Saint James's Palace. In the Eastern church, at Epiphany, the holy water is blessed, a ritual customarily taking place on Holy Saturday (the day before Easter) in the Roman Catholic church. "Epiphany," Microsoft (R) Encarta. Copyright (c) 1994 Microsoft Corporation. Copyright (c) 1994 Funk & Wagnall's Corporation.

Not much help. "Napier" was little better:

Napier, John (1550-1617), Scottish mathematician, born in Merchiston Castle in Edinburgh, and educated at the University of St. Andrews. He became an adherent of the Reformation movement in Scotland while still at college, and in later years he took an active part in Protestant political affairs. He was the author of A Plaine Discovery of the Whole Revelation of Saint John (1593), the first important Scottish interpretation of the Bible.
Napier is best known as the inventor of the first system of logarithms, described in Canonis Descriptio (1614). The common and natural systems of logarithms used today do not employ the same base as Napier's logarithms, although natural logarithms are sometimes called Napierian logarithms. Napier was one of the first, if not the first, to use the decimal point in expressing decimal fractions in a systematic way

and according to the modern system of decimal notation. He also invented mechanical systems for performing arithmetical computations, described in Rabdologia (1617). "Napier, John," Microsoft (R) Encarta. Copyright (c) 1994 Microsoft Corporation. Copyright (c) 1994 Funk & Wagnall's Corporation.

Perhaps the epiphany machine was a mechanical device for settling the vexed question of when Christ was born or how long it was until the apocalypse?

Back in my room I took the bottle out of the bag and poured a generous tot into the tooth mug. Burns claimed that freedom and whisky went together: my recent experiences suggested their disjunction. I found *River out of Eden*, got undressed and into bed, read to the bottom of the glass and put the light off.

I slept fitfully. The TV didn't go off until after two a.m. and there was endless noise from the plumbing.

The sun and I rose around seven thirty. I dressed and went to join the canteen breakfast queue. There was no sign of the Afghani woman.

I was finishing off a bowl of fresh fruit salad when the immigration officer appeared, a small man in a grey suit in tow.

"Would you come to reception as soon as you're ready," she said. "Mr Forsyth has come in especially to see you."
"I'll come now," said I, following them out of the canteen.

"Do come in," said the immigration officer, unlocking the reception office.

She and I sat down at the desk.

"Well," said Mr Forsyth, sitting opposite me, "I've looked at your British passport. As it was issued in Glasgow you're certainly entitled to Scots citizenship but we'll need to sort out some formalities. First of all, where were you born?"

"London," said I.

"Where were your parents born?" said Mr Forsyth.

"London and Ladybrand in South Africa," said I.

"Where were your grandparents born?" said Mr Forsyth.

"England and Eastern Europe," said I. "I've no clues just where though."

"Hmm," said Mr Forsyth. "So you've no familial connection with Scotland. On exactly what grounds are you claiming Scots nationality?"

"But you just said he was entitled to Scots citizenship," said the immigration officer.

"Of course," said Mr Forsyth. "Let me see. How long have you lived in Scotland?"

"Over thirty years," said I.

"Continuously?" said Mr Forsyth.

"No," said I. "I went back to England to study."

"I see," said Mr Forsyth. "So what exactly is your allegiance to Scotland?"

"What do you mean?" said I. "I'm a dual national."

"So why didn't you apply for a Scots passport after liberation?" said Mr Forsyth.

"I didn't think I'd need one," said I. "The treaty said that both sides would recognise the other's passports."

"That wasn't very patriotic of you," said Mr Forsyth. "Don't you want to be Scots?"

"But I am Scots," said I. "Also British. What's the problem?"

"No problem," said Mr Forsyth, reaching into his brief case and pulling out a laptop computer. He unfolded it onto the table and swung out the camera boom. "Smile please!"

The camera flashed.

"Can I have his passport, please?" said Mr Forsyth. The immigration officer passed it over. Mr Forsyth wiped the back page over the scanner above the screen. The computer whirred away, finally ejecting a card from below the keyboard.

"Here you are," said Mr Forsyth. "One Scottish passport, good for a week. You'd better renew it as soon as you get back."
"Thank you," said I. "Can I leave now?"
"Indeed you may," said the immigration officer. "Thank you for your co-operation."
"Can I have my British passport back, please?" said I.
"Oh yes," said Mr Forsyth absently, extracting it from an inside pocket. "Are you sure you'll still need it?"
"Quite sure!" said I.

I gathered my things together, returned the trunks, towel and toiletries to the stores, and walked down the drive to the main gate. The guard inspected my new proof of belonging and opened the gate.

Was I surprised to see Felix waving from the driver's seat of an extended family size Volvo? Not very.

"Get in! " he said, through the open window. "We don't have all day."
"How did you know I'd be here?" said I, complying.
"Robin rang late last night, worried that you hadn't come back," said Felix, accelerating. "This morning I phoned the airline who said that you hadn't taken the flight even though you'd checked in. Swiss immigration said you were here and the office said you were about to be released. Have you got the parcel?"
"I posted it to myself," said I.

"I hope it turns up," said Felix. "There'll be major grief if it doesn't."
"But it's just a book," said I.
"Not 'just a book'," said Felix. "That book's irreplaceable."
"What happened to the man in the cafe?" said I.
"He got a huge erection," said Felix. "I asked him if it was fear or desire but I couldn't hear his answer. When I reckoned you'd had a good enough start I got off him. By then he'd creamed himself. Such a waste."
"Did you get any sense out of him?" said I.
"He said he was a private detective," said Felix, "and he'd been hired by some woman you'd slighted. He claimed he'd information about you that you wouldn't want her to know and he thought he could come to some accommodation with you."

I said nothing.

"Won't you trust me after all I've done for you?" said Felix.

I said nothing. Where to begin? Repetition becomes tiresome.

"There's been a car on our tail since we left Yverdon," said Felix, finally. "I could always just stop if you'd rather."
"Why are you so interested in me?" said I.
"I like you!" said Felix. "But you're not indispensable. I've lots of other potential playmates."

Dissemble? White lie? Selective amnesia? Economy with truth? I certainly wasn't in any hurry to meet up with the customer again.

"I really came here to confront the woman he mentioned," said I. "She abandoned me. Then he turned up and told me she was here. It turns out they're in league together."
"Are they lovers?" said Felix.

"I've no idea," said I.

"Do you still love her?" said Felix.

"Yes," said I. "No. I don't know. Does it matter?"

"Of course it does!" said Felix. "You don't want to end up like Biggles, hard hearted and asexual, if not closeted, after the woman you love turns out to be an enemy agent."

"So where's your Bianca Castafiore?" said I.

"I prefer rough diamonds to emeralds," said Felix.

"Not Algie or Colonel Raymond?" said I.

"Upper class twits," said Felix. "Ginger's more my type."

"I don't know whether to be flattered or insulted," said I.

"Flattered!" said Felix.

"Are they still behind us?" said I.

"No," said Felix, "turned off ages ago."

At the next garage, Felix left the road and drew up on the forecourt.

"I must have some chocolate," he said. "It's been nearly two hours since breakfast. Do you want anything?"

"No thanks," said I.

I waited in the car. He returned shortly, clutching a large brown paper bag which he passed over to me.

"Feed me some chocolate," he said, starting the engine. "And then you could light me a cigarette. Have some yourself if you like."

I looked in the bag and pulled out the English language local paper. Her photograph was on the front cover: "Woman dies in mysterious circumstances." Her photograph.

This is all happening too quickly.

"You could have a look at the film pages for me," said Felix. "They list all the foreign ones and usually say if they're subtitled."

I scanned the article. No mention of anyone else. Body found by cleaning lady early evening. No evidence of foul play. No identification. Post mortem.

I was so exhausted I was past caring. No I wasn't.

I found the cigarette packet, unpeeled the cellophane, engaged the dash board lighter, put two cigarettes in my mouth, lit them, and passed one to Felix, holding it at eye level above the steering wheel.

"You've done that before," said Felix.
"Hitch hiking," said I. "A lorry driver taught me."

I drew deeply on the cigarette and inhaled. Waves of dizziness and nausea slowly subsided.

Of course I hadn't meant to kill her. How was I to know the virus had killed the bloke in the bog? It hadn't hurt me. Of course I didn't want to kill her. Didn't want her dead. Just different. Does each man kill the thing he loves? Of course we're all things. What else are we? The coward does it with a kiss…

"Where to, squire?" said Felix.

Airport? Change tickets? Surveillance? Phone first?

"I rather fancy a longer look round your shop," said I. "Just how many floors are there?"
"Wait and see," said Felix.
"Are they really all first editions?" said I.

"All in good time," said Felix. "Where's that chocolate?"

I felt in the bag and drew out a bar of Toblerone. Peeling back the wrapper, I broke off a triangle and passed it to Felix.

"Have some yourself," said Felix.
"No thanks," said I.
"Love drug," said Felix. "Do you good."
"Not just now," said I.
"You're not very chirpy," said Felix.
"I've just spent twenty four hours in an internment camp," said I. "Did you expect me to march through the gates whistling 'Colonel Bogey'?"

Felix burst into song:

> *Prentice has only got one Hall,*
> *Chapman has one but very small,*
> *McGraw has somewhat similar,*
> *But poor old Penguin has no Halls at all...*

"Most droll," said I, smiling in spite of myself.

We bantered our way back to Geneva, Felix with rather more gusto than I. Back in the old town, he parked opposite the shop.

"In we go," said Felix, unlocking the door and releasing the blind. He threw a switch and the comforting gloom returned.

"Shall we start at the bottom?" said Felix, disappearing into the back of the shop. I followed him down to the nineteenth century.

"Come on!" said Felix, already at the far end, descending to the eighteenth century. Strangely, there were as many books on this floor as on the two above.

"Are you still with me?" said Felix, once more at the back of the shop on the stairs to the seventeenth century.
"I don't believe this!" said I, torn between browsing and keeping up.

"Nearly there," said Felix, passing the downwards sign at the front of the shop.

The sixteenth century was different. Very different. The room was empty, apart from a large oak chest directly under a naked light bulb in the centre, bound with studded iron bands and secured with a padlock.

"Here's where it all begins," said Felix.
"So what's in there then?" said I, flustered.
"Books you've only dreamed of," said Felix. "Lost books. Fabulous books. Books that might have been written. Books that only exist in books."
"Oh yes," said I. "Aristotle's book on humour, perchance?"
"Indeed," said Felix. "One of my predecessors sold it to him."
"Your shop sold Aristotle on humour to Umberto Eco?" said I.
"No, not Eco," said Felix. "Borges. Where do you think Eco got the idea from?"
"But Eco's William of Baskerville," said I.
"Not at all," said Felix. "He's just as much Jorge of Burgos. The *Name of the Rose* is all about the cosmic battle between rationalism and mysticism. Eco's a magic realist through and through."
"But magic realism's all Catholic," said I.
"No no no," said Felix. "Magic realism's relative to any world view. Most science fiction's atheist magic realism. *Lanark*'s Protestant magic realism. Anyway, the straight religious people in Eco are all ciphers. The interesting stuff's heretical or hermeneutic. Eco's a materialist magic realist so his magic

fits each character according to their ideology."

"What other monstrous fabrications have you palmed off?" said I, incredulous.

"Well," said Felix, "the owner before that sold Lenin volume five of *Das Kapital*."

"Marx only wrote three volumes," said I, "though I suppose some people do claim that *Theories of Surplus Value*'s really volume four."

"Volume five's about the organisation of communist economies," said Felix.

"So what was in the parcel you gave me?" said I.

There was a noise from above. Footsteps on the spiral staircase.

"There they are!" shouted the customer. "You won't get away this time!"

Felix drew a large key from his waistcoat pocket, undid the padlock and threw back the lid.

"Quick!" he said. "Get in! I'll hold them off as long as I can."

I peered over the edge of the chest from which an even golden light shone. A ladder stretched downwards. Without hesitating, I climbed in and started down. Felix shut the lid above me. The ladder ended three metres below at the start of a corridor. At the far end was a door. To the left, an alcove held a telephone. A red light blinked on the hand piece. I picked it up.

"Thank you for choosing Timeline," said the androgynous mid-Atlantic voice. "When instructed, select one to reverse time; select two to bifurcate time; select three to freeze time. Select now, please."

I pushed `3`, playing for time.

"You have selected freeze time," said the voice. "You now have twenty minutes in which everything except yourself will not change. Timeline cannot accept responsibility for the consequences of your actions during this period. You have not been charged for this call. Thank you for choosing Timeline."

A large analogue clock set to twenty minutes lit up on the wall above the phone, the second hand moving inexorably anti-clockwise.

I raced along the corridor and clambered up the ladder but the lid was rigid. I tumbled back down and pushed on the door which opened out of the folds in John Knox's nether regions onto the plaza in front of the Reformation Monument.

Everything was still. It had been windy and the flag over the University was rippled starch stiff. Leaves hovered twixt branch and broom. All around, nothing moved and there was no sound. People transfixed mid-step, mid-cough, mid-kiss.

Suspending time is low risk for paradoxes. You can't murder your own father or seduce your own mother or engage in other troubling Oedipal activities. All it does is give you a head start on what's going to happen anyway.

I ran through the park past the frozen chess players, up the hill onto the terrace and back into the shop.

The seconds ticked by as I wheezed down through the ages: twentieth century, nineteenth century, eighteenth century, seventeenth century.

The bottom floor held a tableau worthy of a sixteenth century masque. Felix lay back across the box, his left arm thrown up to ward off the blow from the customer's clenched fist. His companion stood to one side, in the shadows, watching. I toppled the customer over and eased Felix onto the floor. Check the watch. Seven minutes left. I opened the lid and in a manic flood of adrenaline poured Felix into the chest, followed him down and pulled the lid shut behind us.

At the bottom of the ladder, Felix looked at me quizzically. "You took your time," he said.
"I took your time," said I. "What the hell happens now?"
"I need to make a quick call," said Felix, hastening to the phone. "Where would you like to go to?"
"Home sounds nice," said I.
"When?" said Felix.
"Now?" said I.
"Fine," said Felix, and spoke into the mouthpiece. "Have you got any plastic?"
"Book Token charge card?" said I, fossicking in a pocket and inspecting the first to come to hand.
"Pass it over," said Felix. "I hope they give air miles."

He swiped the card into the phone base.

"Looks like they've accepted it," said Felix. "Just go through the door."
"What about you?" said I.
"Oh, I'll be all right," said Felix. "Give us a ring when you get back, why don't you?"
"Indeed I will," said I. "Thanks!"
"For nothing," said Felix. "I just hope you're a bit less inhibited next time."
"Fidgee fidgee," said I, pushing the door open.
"Boodle boodle," said Felix.

4. On the hill

I entered a kaleidoscopic maelstrom? An endless dark tunnel? The tangled madnesses of my entire life relived simultaneously? A vast white expanse?

The men's toilets beneath the east entrance to the old Royal Infirmary. A locked cubicle, walls covered with drawings demonstrating a direct lineage between our culture and Pompeii's. The attendant double took as I walked past him and up the steps to the top of Middle Meadow Walk.

I looked at the clock above *The Doctors*. Six p.m. Four hours lost somewhere, even allowing for the time shift between Scotland and the rest of Europe. Napier's bones. What to do? Find Robin. Find the Professor. Pass the parcel.

North along Forest Road and down Candlemaker Row to the bookshop. Shut. Back into the Grassmarket and up the close. Gate locked. Along to the Vennel, up the steps, round the Art College, across the road and down to the west end of the Meadows.

Sodium street light on bare budded branches; yellow stellations through thick lurking haar; crisp frosted grass crunching under my feet.

I found my keys and opened the front door. The corridor was lined ceiling high with cardboard boxes. The kitchen sink was piled with dirty dishes. Clothes were strewn across the sitting room, a sleeping bag on the sofa. No toilet paper. No hot water. No parcel. No Professor. Probably in the pub. I felt a sudden urge for a pint.

The *Earl of Marchmont* used be *The Totem*, unpretentious and full of students: it's still full of students. The Professor was in the far corner staring vacantly into an empty glass. I bought two pints of IPA and joined him.

"Oh!" said the Professor. "You're back! What've you done to your beard?"

I stroked my chin. Clean shaven. But I'd no recollection of shaving.

"What have you done to my flat?" said I, sitting down and passing him a pint.
"You said I could move in," said the Professor.
"You said you didn't have any stuff," said I.
"Ah," said the Professor. "She's got temporary possession of the house until the sharks finalise things."
"How long for?" said I.
"Could be a couple of months," said the Professor. "Do you mind?"
"We'll see," said I. "Did a packet arrive for me."
"Oh yes," said the Professor. "Marked 'Urgent!'. I took it to work."
"Did you open it?" said I.
"Of course I opened it!" said the Professor. "Just an old book."
"Just an old book?" said I. "I hope it's somewhere safe."
"Of course it is," said the Professor.
"Any progress on the file?" said I.
"Well," said the Professor, "I'm still getting possibilities from Australia but there's actually an absurd number of six letter phrases and they're all equally plausible. So I began to think about them as arbitrary encodings rather than text. That's where it all gets a bit weird."
"Weird?" said I.
"Weird," said the Professor.
"How weird?" said I.
"Life the universe and everything weird," said the Professor.
"Oh come on!" said I.

"No," said the Professor, "I'm serious. Have you got a bit of paper?"
"There's lots of beer mats," said I.
"Look," said the Professor, taking out a propelling pencil, "we can view six lots of eight bit bytes in a surprising number of different ways. First of all, they can encode mathematical expressions as well as text."
"What do you mean?" said I.

Gentle reader: if you don't like squiggly stuff then do skip three pages or so.

The Professor wrote down six numbers.

"Take out the spaces in between and what have you got?" said the Professor.
"One big number," said I.
"What we call a Gödel number," said the Professor. "Suppose we see how often we can divide it by 2, and then by 3 and then by 5 and then by 7 and then by 11 and then by 13 and so on."
"Those are all prime numbers," said I.
"Indeed," said the Professor. "What do we get?"
"Lots of new numbers," said I.
"Suppose each of those new numbers is a code for a symbol," said the Professor.
"Message in a bottle," said I. "What's that spell?"

$$\{x \mid x \notin x\}$$

wrote the Professor.

"The set of all x," said I, "such that x is not a member of itself. Russell's paradox."

"Right," said the Professor. "Now, if we do a different decoding we get..." and wrote down:

$(\lambda\ s.s\ s)$

"Explain," said I.

"Lambda calculus," said the Professor. "That's the function that applies its argument to its argument."

"Eh?" said I.

"You can read it as 'replace *s* in *s s*'," said the Professor. "Suppose we write it down next to itself..." and wrote down:

$(\lambda\ s.s\ s)\ (\lambda\ s.s\ s)$

"Reading from left to right, that says 'replace *s* in *s s* with $(\lambda\ s.s\ s)$'" said the Professor. "We replace the first *s* with $(\lambda\ s.s\ s)$ giving..." and wrote down:

$(\lambda\ s.s\ s)$

"...and then replace the second *s* with... $(\lambda\ s.s\ s)$" and wrote down another $(\lambda\ s.s\ s)$ next to the first one:

$(\lambda\ s.s\ s)\ (\lambda\ s.s\ s)$

"But that's what you started with!" said I.

"Precisely!" said the Professor. "It just reproduces itself endlessly!"

I said nothing.

"Anyway," said the Professor, "with a different encoding we get a Turing machine quintuplet..." and wrote down:

`0 _ 1 R 0`

"This is gobbledegook!" said I.

"Not at all," said the Professor. "A Turing machine's got a tape made up of cells. Each cell starts off blank and can hold a symbol like a *0* or a *1*. The machine starts off over a cell, looks at it, changes it and then moves left or right. The quintuplets are instructions that say what the machine's to do at each stage. You can read this one as saying 'in state *o*, if the cell's *blank* then put a *1* in it, move *right* to the next cell, and stay in state *o* for the next action'. Suppose this is our initial tape with every cell blank. We start with the machine in state 0, looking at the leftmost cell..."

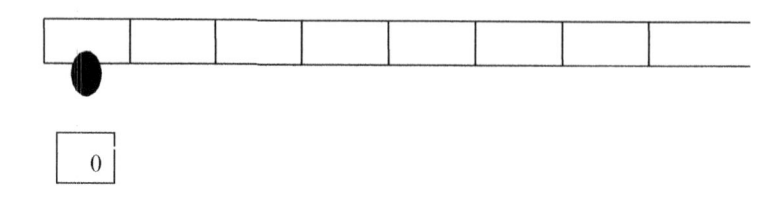

"The cell's blank so the machine writes a *1*, moves right and stays in state *0*..."

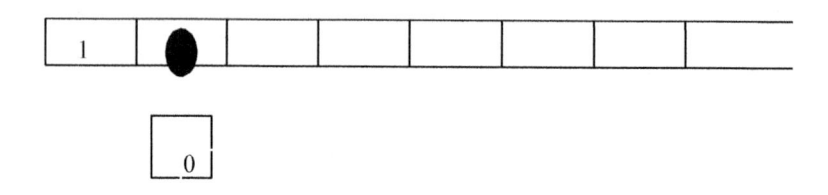

"The cells blank so it writes a *1*, moves right and stays in state *o*..."

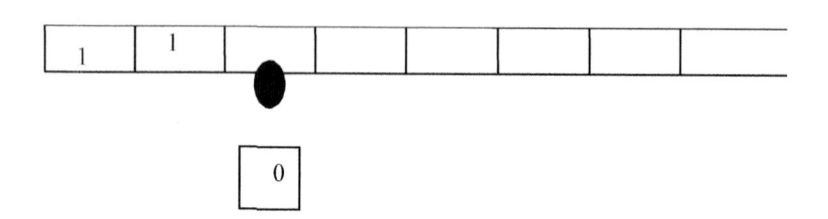

"So it goes on writing *1*'s," said I, "until it runs out of cells."
"Oh no," said the Professor, "the tape's infinite."
"You can't have an infinite tape," said I.
"No," said the Professor. "It's a gedanken experiment. Anyway, suppose we try another encoding..." and wrote down:

    n -> 1 n

"So?" said I.

"It's a Chomsky regular expression," said the Professor. "It says 'everywhere there's an n, replace it with $1\ n$'. Let's start with n..." and wrote down:

    `n`

"which we replace with $1\ n$..." and wrote down:

    `1n`

"and then we replace n with $1\ n$..." and wrote down:

    `11n`

"and then we replace n with $1\ n$..." and wrote down:

    `111n`

"It never stops!" said I, grabbing the propelling pencil from him. "Absolutely!" said the Professor.

Almost the end of the squiggles.

"What's your point?" said I.
"Doesn't it seem a bit strange that six seemingly arbitrary numbers encode endless sequences in different formalisms?" said the Professor.

There are no coincidences. A conspiracy of computability confabulists? There are no conspiracies.

"Russell's paradox isn't an endless sequence," said I.
"Of course it is!" said the Professor. "Think about a computer's filing system. It's made up of a hierarchy of folders with links to files and other folders. On some systems a folder can have a link back to itself. In principle, we could

look at each folder in turn and see if it's got a link to itself or not. Then we could make up a new folder with links to all the folders that don't have links to themselves. Now, does that folder have a link to itself? If it doesn't then we better give it a link to itself but now it's got a link to itself so we better remove the link to itself so now it doesn't have a link to itself so we better give it a link to itself, and so on."

Suddenly I felt very tired.

"You're enjoying this, aren't you?" said I.
"Sure beats marking first year exams," said the Professor.
"I'm awa hame," said I. "I'm really hungry. Are you coming?"
"I was going to go back to work," said the Professor. "I'll see you later, maybe."

When I got back to the flat something felt amiss. The boxes were still in the hall; clothes still littered the sitting room; the sink was still solidifying. But it was as if everything had been picked up and put down again. Suddenly I realised that all the book spines were flush with the fronts of the shelves. I always push them hard back to the wall to make it easier to get them in and out. Books are for reading, not for an impressive array of titles. Anxiously I checked the rows. Nothing appeared to be missing, not even my first edition of *The Green Child*. Now there's a book. Out of print though you can occasionally find the Penguin Modern Classic with the Max Ernst cover.

I went into my bedroom. On close inspection, all the cupboards and drawers had been opened and the contents returned to not quite the right places. But everything was still there.

Yes, yes, the parcel from Felix. Well, the Professor did say he had it somewhere safe. What did I care. I was very tired indeed. And hungry. Sod the bones.

I phoned the Himalaya and ordered a home delivery: pakura; chicken tikka; vegetable massallam; garlic nan. Next I stacked the clothes and the contents of the sink onto the sleeping bag. The food arrived promptly. Hot and spicy. I wolfed it down. Replete, I moused up the email. A solitary message from Robin urging me to contact her as soon as I got back. Yes, yes, gifts from Geneva. Time to sleep.

At around two a.m. I woke briefly to muffled curses and the sound of running water.

At eight a.m., I felt much revived. No sign of the Professor but the sitting room and kitchen were spotless. I showered, dressed, breakfasted and headed off across the Meadows.

Tai Chi, cherry trees; sun rise over Arthur's Seat; dog turds on dead leaves.

The shop was open. Robin was at the front desk.
"Are you all right?" she said as I entered.
"Just fine!" said I.
"I got worried when you didn't show up so I called Felix," said Robin. "What exactly happened?"

Repetition becomes tiresome. It's absurd how long we spend telling different people the same stories, telling the same people different stories.

"... so Felix picked me up and took me straight to the airport," I finished.
"Have you got the book he gave you?" said Robin.
"I posted it back to myself from the camp," said I. "I didn't know how long I'd be banged up for."
"Has it arrived?" said Robin.
"Not yet," said I. "Why is it so important?"

"Did Felix explain what we're doing?" said Robin.
"Not in so many words," said I.
"Ah," said Robin.
"Why didn't you ever tell me you were dealing in antiquarian books?" said I. "It must be far more lucrative than all this stuff."
"How do you think I keep the shop going?" said Robin. "You know how much we make."
"I always assumed you had some sort of private income," said I.

Robin laughed.

"So what's the book Felix gave me?" I persisted.
"The only extant copy of John Napier's journal," said Robin.

Oh yes.

"Surely Felix can get you another," said I.

Robin looked puzzled.

"What do you mean?" said Robin. "I told you, it's the only copy."
"Right," said I. "Who's it for then?"
"The man you were serving before lunch last Thursday," said Robin.

Oh yes.

"Well who is he then?" said I.
"I've got his details in the order book," said Robin. "What does it matter?"
"Curiosity," said I. "Anyway, why did you tell me that coming in today was all right if the books were so important?"
"He came back in on Saturday and was very pushy," said Robin. "There's a lot of money involved."

"How much lots?" said I.

"Lots lots," said Robin.

"You don't trust your courier," said I.

"You don't trust your friends," said Robin.

"What do you mean?" said I.

"You went to Geneva to see her, didn't you," said Robin.

"How do you know that?" said I.

"She phoned me last night," said Robin.

Bloody hell! How much does it cost to buy a front page headline in a Swiss daily? There are no conspiracies. Maybe it was the only extant copy?

"Last night?" said I.

"Yes, last night," said Robin. "First time for ages. She said she'd hoped you could make it up with each other but it didn't work out."

"Napier's bones," said I.

"There's probably something about them in his journal," said Robin. "Look, I'd really appreciate it if you could check if the book's turned up. I suppose I haven't been totally up front with you. We can talk through the arrangements with Felix and you can take on some of the ordering. After all, you know what he's like now."

"Indeed I do," said I. "Does he only proposition men?"

"He does not," said Robin, "but I think it's a psychic tic rather than serious."

"I'll go and look after lunch," said I.

"Thanks," said Robin. "To work then?"

"I see the replacement's arrived," said I, gesticulating towards the shiny new computer. "Do you want me to set it up?"

"Please," said Robin. "You backed it all up at the end of the month, didn't you?"

"Certainly did," said I, looking under the desk. "And they didn't find the disks."

I spent a dull morning inserting CDs and reconstructing the sales monitoring system. We'd lost a week's details but we could always reconcile stock against distributors' invoices if we had to.

At lunch time I went back to the Grassmarket to look for the Professor. He wasn't in his lab and there was no sign of the parcel. A student told me that he'd gone off with two of his research assistants up Blackford Hill.

No time to lose. I flagged down a cab which dropped me at the car park for the National Observatory, beyond the former University of Edinburgh's science campus.

I walked up the slope towards the Ordinance Survey marker. A clear, raw day. Brisk easterly wind. I'm still puzzled about the names for wind directions. A south wind is from the south but a southerly wind sounds like it should be towards the south, as in 'blow the wind southerly', by analogy with 'they went in a southerly direction'. I looked 'southerly' up once: the dictionary said that it means both 'from the south' and 'towards the south'.

On top of the hill, a broad panorama: to the east, the whale bone arch on Berwick Law; to the west, the snowy peaks of the Trossachs; across the city to the Forth and Fife and the Ochils and the Lomonds. Carved into the marker pedestal, the rallying cry against the dead hand of Cartesian dualism: "Polar co-ordinates rule OK".

There I found a most excited The Professor, peering towards Arthur's Seat through binoculars and talking animatedly into a mobile phone.

"... to the left a bit ... over a bit ... yes, try there..."

Of course his name isn't really 'The Professor'. For a start he isn't a Professor. Years ago we had a summer job on the night shift in the Inglis Green laundry and he suggested replacing a Taylorist allocation of one task to one individual with small groups who followed batches of clothes right through the whole process. The shift leader had been there for years and mocked his presumption until we completed the evening's quota in two thirds of the usual time. From then on it was: 'what does the Professor think?'. So, how to refer to him? Perhaps '… an excited Professor, …'? But which Professor? The Professor!

"Have a look!" said the Professor, turning round and passing me the binoculars.
"What am I looking for? said I.
"On top of Samson's Ribs," said the Professor.
"Oh yes," said I. "Itch and Scratchit. Is digging in their contracts?"
"Pass them back!" said the Professor.

"… any sign of anything yet?…"

Itch and Scratchit were inseparable. Of indeterminate gender and ethnic origin, they accompanied each other everywhere. They'd met as undergraduates and had stayed on in the Professor's department, first as postgraduate students and then as researchers.

Almost silent in each other's company, they were rumoured to be telepathic. They spent their waking hours in the laboratory, in the obligatory nest of soft drink cans and fast food containers: the safety committee had turned down their request to install hammocks.

What exactly they researched was not entirely clear though undoubtedly cutting edge. They were certainly hard working, churning out endless variants on the same paper, all with the Professor as first author.

"… Yes it's bloody cold! I'm bloody cold! We're all bloody cold! …"

It was plain that they despised the Professor, yet they seemed curiously fond of him, as if comforted by his limited grasp of their rich inner world. He found them research grants and they put up with his occasional foibles.

"... you've hit something? What sort of something?..."

"What's going on?" said I.
"Napier's bones!" said the Professor. "It's all in his note book! There's a map showing a rainbow connecting Arthur's Seat and Blackford Hill. He could only see that if the sun was way behind Merchiston Tower. You can just about see the Tower from here but there's no way you can see Arthur's Seat from there now with all the new buildings."
"What are you looking for?" said I.
"Treasure!" said the Professor.
"At the end of the rainbow?" said I. "Come on!"
"Absolutely!" said the Professor. "Napier had a reputation as a sorcerer. He's supposed to have entered an agreement with Robert Logan of Restalrig to look for treasure at Fastcastle round the coast from North Berwick."
"What do you mean 'supposed'?" said I.
"Remember books?" said the Professor. "You sell them, no? I went to the Central Library and found a biography. Really badly written but a mine of what little info's available. I bet you didn't know that he's supposed to have built an infernal device which could clear an area four miles round of all living things."
"An epiphany machine?" said I.
"Only if you regard entropy as epiphany," said the Professor.
"So why aren't you digging here then?" said I.
"The map's divided into squares." said the Professor. "If you use the numbers from the file you found as a grid reference then they point straight at Samson's Ribs!"

But that's the only extant copy of Napier's journals. So where did the map reference come from?

The Professor squinted through the binoculars.

"…what've you found?… a box?… we'll come straight over… don't open it…"

An immense explosion shook the hill. Sheets of flame rose from Samson's Ribs.

"Not so good," said the Professor.
"We'd better get over there," said I.
"Don't be daft, man!" said the Professor. "The place'll be crawling with police. Do you feel like trying to explain what's happened?"
"Come on!" said I. "How did you get here?"
"In my car," said the Professor. "I dropped them at the foot of the Ribs on my way over."

Turning to go, I saw the customer staggering slowly up the hill, panting furiously.

"I'll see you later!" said I.
"Where are you going?" said the Professor.
"Whatever happens, you don't know me," said I.
"If you say so," said the Professor.

I headed south west away from the car park, slipping on the steep muddy path down to the base of the hill. Round past the pond. On Sundays we used to come and feed the ducks with the week's stale bread. Out of the park onto the main road and up through the Grange to Marchmont.

Why was I running? Fear. Anyway I was walking. Where was I going? Home?

But that's where they'd go to look for me. Fear of what? Humiliation and violence? They? Both of them? Was she really alive? Robin said so. Of course I trusted Robin. How did he know I was on the hill? There are no coincidences.

A code carrying virus. An undecodable file. A priceless journal. Plain as Pike's staff.

I went back to the shop.

"Any joy?" said Robin.
"There's been a mix up with the courier," said I. "I need to go over to Sighthill to unscramble things. I can't do it by phone, they need my signature."
"Off you go then," said Robin.
"Has your customer been back yet?" said I.
"He was here just after you left," said Robin. "I told him we'd try and have the books by this evening. He said he'd go for a walk and come back at closing time. I suggested Blackford Hill. The view's amazing on a day like this."
"Certainly is," said I.

I went back to the lab. The Professor was at his desk.

"Are they all right?" said I.
"A bit singed," said the Professor. "The bomb squad said they'd found an old box of thunder flashes. Apparently Hunter's Bog used to be a firing range and there are stashes of explosives all over the hillside."
"What about your treasure?" said I.

The Professor reached into a desk drawer and pulled out a brown paper bag.

"Have a look," he said.

I poured the bag onto the desk.

"Roman coins," said I.

"Gold," said the Professor. "The explosion unearthed them. They gathered them up before the law arrived. They said they'd been metal detecting, which isn't entirely untrue. I'll get them valued at the Museum the morn'."

"Don't they want them? " said I.

"Didn't seem very interested," said the Professor.

"Can I have the book?" said I.

"Sure," said the Professor. "I'll get it for you."

"Can I photocopy it here?" said I.

"I did that yesterday," said the Professor.

"Have you got the Napier biography?" said I.

"I've no library tickets," said the Professor, "but no one's had it out for ages so it'll still be there. There's something strange about this journal though. According to the book, Napier's papers were lost when some descendant's house burnt down."

"Oh yes," said I.

The Professor went off to find the book. I nosed round the laboratory. Nothing ever seemed to change. Along the back wall was the history of human-computer interaction. In the far corner a cardpunch. Next to it, a teletype, upper-case only, with integral printer and paper tape reader/punch. Then an early Visual Display Unit, screen dwarfed by the casing, again upper-case only. The next VDU had lower-case as well. The next had cursor keys. Now a series of microcomputers. The ubiquitous Commodore Pet, all metal, Darth Vader screen enclosure, built-in cassette recorder, calculator style square keys. A Cromenco with a single density 8 inch floppy drive. A North Star Horizon with a double density 5.25 inch drive. A twin drive IBM PC. A shiny black Sinclair QL and an Apple II and a BBC micro and a Macintosh with the tiny screen that cried out for a fresnel lens. A PC AT clone made by some long forgotten UK manufacturer with double density 5.25 inch and 3 inch floppy drives. At last the workstations. A Perq with a portrait A4 black and white screen. A VAX station. A colour Sun 3, probably still serviceable if somewhat slow.

"Why don't you clear this lot out?" I said as the Professor returned clutching the parcel. "Give it all to a museum. There are probably people who collect this stuff."

"Nostalgia. Heritage. Educational value. Laziness. Avarice," said the Professor. "Here you go."

I took the parcel, opened it and took out the Napier journal.

"There are some pages missing," said the Professor.
"Which ones?" said I.
"It's mostly in Latin, so I kept the ones in English," said the Professor.
"You tore pages out of a four hundred year old book?" I said. "Are you mad? Why couldn't you just photocopy them?"
"It's only a book," said the Professor. "Anyway, it's really tatty already. No one'll notice."
"It's not only a book!" said I.
"The holy church of the written word?" said the Professor. "Call yourself an atheist!"
"Give!" said I.
"Shan't!" said the Professor. "What are you going to do with them? Sellotape them back in? That'll look authentic."
"It's cold in a cardboard box at this time of year," said I.
"Oh very well then," said the Professor, sheepishly. "Do you want them right now?"
"No," said I. "I'll deliver the book first and come back for them."
"Right you are then," said the Professor.

5. In the museum

I went back up Candlemaker Row, past the shop, onto George IVth Bridge, across to Chamber St to the National Museum of Scotland. I could hardly go straight back to Robin having told her I was off to Sighthill. Anyway, I thought that the Museum might have a John Napier display.

I strode up the steps and through the revolving doors. The main hall and tiered display galleries were bathed in natural light from the high glass roof.

"Are you Scottish?" said the woman on the entrance desk.

Proudly I flourished my shiny new passport.

"In you go then," she said, swiping it into the till.
"What about a British passport?" said I.
"Only if it were issued in Glasgow," said the woman.

A nation once again.

"Is there a gallery for mathematics?" said I.
"I'm afraid not," said the woman. "What are you looking for?"
"John Napier," said I.
"Try the mediatheque," said the woman.
"What's a mediatheque?" said I.
"We used to call it the library," said the woman, "but everythings's on-line now."

Page | 77

"I like books," said I.

"So do I," said the woman, sadly. "Third floor."

The mediateque was at the very back of the building in what used to be the science and engineering display. I'd come here in wet school lunch breaks: touch the van der Graff generator case with one hand and the radiator with other, and jump at the shocks; worry about being red-green colour blind when I couldn't see the '42' supposedly lurking amongst the shimmering coloured dots; watch the planets rotating slowly on the huge mechanical orrery; lean over the balcony and try and catch the wire for the Foucault pendulum. The Foucault's pendulum?

All gone. No more glass cabinets full of unfathomable technologies with terse labels. Instead a row of ubiquitous chips, each with its own VR head-set. Nobody else in sight. I sat down at the first workplace, introductory screen inviting interaction, buttoned my way past the messages from our sponsors, selected Search, typed:

Napier's bones

into the obliging box and hit the Return key. Someone had done their homework. A soothing Scots female voice talked through the animation...

Napier's bones are an early system for simplifying multiplication. The bones are actually rectangular rods, each one inscribed with the times table for the numbers 0 to 9... <see Appendix 1>

To educate and entertain. Lord Reith would be proud. But no clues as to the cosmic significance of two words scrawled on a piece of paper at the bottom of a tin of cigars. I menued my way back to the Search option and tried:

epiphany machine

So what did I expect? At best nothing. At worst a general protection fault. Certainly not:

Welcome to the epiphany machine.
Please enter your password:

Amazed, I typed in:

Napier's bones
Password invalid. Returning to host system.

Desperately I selected the search option again, re-entered:

epiphany machine

and tried:

napiersbones

at the password prompt:

Password invalid. Returning to host system.

How many more password failures would the system tolerate before someone was notified about a hacker manqué? Stop and think. The file on the organiser. Of course I hadn't written down the Gödel number the Professor showed me in the pub. Take the book back to Robin. Find the Professor. Find the undecodable code.

I wimped back to the entry screen, picked up the book and left.

The shop shutter was up but the light was still on. I let myself in. No sign of Robin but a note on the desk:

Gone home. Please phone. Love R

I dialled her number:

"Hi Robin, it's me."
"Yes, it's here."
"When's he coming round?"
"OK, I'll be straight over."

… and hung up. I shut up the shop and headed along the Grassmarket, up the steps to Johnstone Terrace and the Esplanade, down Ramsay Lane and the Mound, past the Galleries, across Princes Street onto Hanover Street.

Robin and I go back a long way. We never made love, never even had sex, just good friends. No she's really not scheming and manipulative. Of course she's what they used to call a control freak. Aren't we all?

Robin lived in the top floor of what was originally a double upper flat, on Queen Street. The windows come down to about a foot off the floor: the views north are quite magnificent. South facing stone tiled kitchen full of plants; beeswaxed oak table and wheel backed chairs. Bedroom wall to wall books, mostly fiction and poetry; single bed. Sitting room sparse: white walls, sanded floor, beaming brass Buddha by the door, wooden Swedish armchairs with cream woven upholstery, cushions in the bay window - Robin liked to sit there cross legged reading or writing or gazing out absently. Past tense? Indeed. Is 'presently' the opposite of 'absently'?

I rang the entry phone and Robin buzzed me in.

"Do come in," said Robin, opening the door at the top of the stair well.
"Thanks," said I, closing it behind.
"Tea?" said Robin, leading me into the kitchen. "Weak with lemon?"
"Sounds good!" said I.
"Is that the book?" said Robin.

I passed it to her.

"Glad to be shot of it," said I.
"Do sit down," said Robin, "I'll just fill the kettle."
"No, let me," said I.

I topped up the kettle and plugged it in while Robin lightly dusted the inside of the pot with Earl Gray.

"There's something I need to tell you," said Robin, pouring the gnats piss into two hand thrown mugs.
"Fire away," said I, taking one.
"You know the shop's not been doing so well," said Robin.
"Indeed," said I.
"Something's got to be done," said Robin.
"Business process re-engineering?" said I.
"Not exactly," said Robin.
"Not exactly?" said I. "How not exactly?"
"I'm going to close the shop," said Robin, "but I want to expand the mail order first editions."
"Why now?" said I.
"You know it's always bad after Christmas," said Robin, "'til the tourists come back in April. Last Christmas was really lousy, after the SNP's austerity programme to keep up with the pound. We can only pay the bills for another couple of weeks. I'd rather go out on a high."

"Why not go on subsidising the shop with the old books?" said I. "I thought you believed in providing a community resource."

"What community?" said Robin. "Our customers are ageing at the same rate as us."

"So what's the deal with Felix?" said I.

"Customers approach me," said Robin, "I contact Felix and he sends me the books. Payment is to him. I get five percent."

"Five percent?" said I. "Is that all?"

"Five hundred pounds on the book you just brought," said Robin.

"Five hundred pounds?" I echoed. "Five percent? That's crazy!"

I sipped my tea.

"So why did I have to go to Geneva?" said I. "Why wouldn't special delivery do? It's probably a lot safer. And cheaper."

"The customer insisted that the book be delivered in person," said Robin.

"Did you tell him it would be me who went?" said I.

"He asked if I could go myself and I said that was impossible," said Robin. "He asked if there was anyone else and I mentioned you, which seemed to cheer him up. I thought it might be a way for you to get a break. When you said you were going anyway it seemed too good to be true."

But the customer told me to go in the first place?

"How long have you been thinking about closing for?" said I.

"Quite a while," said Robin.

"Why didn't you say anything earlier?" said I.

"You've been a bit distracted since she left," said Robin. "I didn't want to undermine you any further. Anyway, I've been getting more and more sick of it. I like buying books to read, not to sell to other people."

"You're really that fed up?", said I.

"Ten years is a long time," said Robin, "and there really is bugger-all to show for it."

"Is there any point in arguing with you?" said I.

"Not unless it makes you feel better," said Robin.

"Where does that leave me?" said I.

"Where do you want to be left?" said Robin.

"I don't suppose there's much chance of redundancy money," said I.

"No," said Robin.

The bell rang.

"That'll be him," said Robin, standing up.

"I'd rather not be involved," said I.

"Fine," said Robin, shutting the door behind her.

I sat and stared into the cup. Why don't I tell someone? Who can I trust? Why don't the three boys turn up and give me the bells?

Raised voices from the hall. I got up. The front door slammed. Robin came back into the kitchen, looking fierce.

"Stroppy bastard!" said Robin.

"What's wrong?" said I.

"He claims it's missing some pages," said Robin. "How the hell does he know how many pages there should be? It's not as if it starts with the contents!"

"Maybe he was expecting to find something in it," said I.

"Tough!" said Robin. "A deal's a deal. He can go and shout at Felix."

We both sat down.

"To come back to the shop…" said I.

"Right!" said Robin. "Do you want to come in on the mail order?"

"What would I do?" said I.

"I don't much care so long as we can sell enough books," said Robin.
"It's not as if you can't handle one book a week perfectly well on your own," said I.
"That one's exceptional," said Robin. "I usually make nearer twenty five pounds."
"That's three times what we make on a hardback," said I.
"Precisely," said Robin. "No overheads either apart from postage and publicity. Lots more time for writing."
"Can I sleep on it?" said I.
"Fine," said Robin. "Take your time. Anyway, how was your trip?"
"Not a whole bundle of fun," said I.
"Do you want to talk about it?" said Robin.

I hate conversations that start: "Do you want to talk about it?". It usually means: "There's obviously something fascinating happening to you and I'd like all the details. Now. Not that I'm nosy…". Of course I like gossiping!

Repetition becomes tiresome.

"…so she said she wasn't ready to come back yet," said I.
"Sounds like what she told me," said Robin.
"Sounds like something out of a women's magazine," said I. "Grieving jilted partner flies to romantic location for tragic but mature resolution."
"Oh come on," said Robin. "It was worth a try. Anyway, you know where you stand now."

Robin's her friend. She phoned Robin. Robin got me to collect the Napier book. But the customer was in Geneva anyway. Why didn't he just get the book from Felix? Why didn't she just get it? She knew that I had to be kissed. Did she know that I was the book courier? Did she know that the book was to be couriered? What does Robin know? What do I know?

"It's funny that she phoned you after such a long time," said I, cautiously. "Have you really not heard anything of her since she left?"

"You know I haven't!" said Robin. "I'd've told you! You know that!"

"Sorry," said I. "I'm really tired and not thinking straight."

"You stupid man!" said Robin affectionately. "Go home and get some sleep!"

She let me out.

"See you the morn'," said I.

"See you the morn'," said Robin.

Weary and hungry. Can't afford to eat this close to Princes Street. Not that I'd want to. It's all 'authentic' Scottish cooking: haggis roulade with a neep vinaigrette. Real Scots subsist on fat, not just black pudding and chips but an international diet: deep fried pizza and curry laced with ghee. Top of the European heart attack league. Cuisine ur-mince.

Can't afford a taxi. By the time I've waited for a bus I might as well have walked it.

Up Frederick Street, over the road into the Gardens. Down the slope to the right of the bandstand, beside the Norwegian memorial boulder and the stepping stones to the ring of Robert Louis Stevenson birch trees. Past the triple layer fountain, over the railway bridge and up round the side of Castle Rock to the bottom of Johnstone Terrace. Down Spittal Street, up Lady Lawson Street and over the West Port. No time to browse Bert's second hand bookshop. Down Chalmers Street past the Eye Pavilion and Thomas of Aquinas School, and onto the Meadows.

The east wind bore burning. When I reached the flat, the fire crew were rolling up the hoses.

"You forgot the journal pages," said the Professor, lurking nervously.
"What happened?" said I, taking them from him.
"God knows," said the Professor. "This lot were here when I got back."
"Are you the owner," said the Fire Investigation Officer.
"I am," said I. "What happened?"
"Too early to tell, " said the Fire Investigation Officer, "but it looks like arson. The fire started near the front door. It's lucky everyone was out and we got here quickly. There's no apparent structural damage so you should be able to move back in fairly soon."
"Can we go in now?" said I.
"Sure," said the Fire Investigation Officer, "but you'll need to talk to the police."

I walked over to the police car.

"You again," said the Sergeant.
"Indeed," said I.
"Let's have your name and address then," said the Sergeant.
"You know both already," said I.
"Just for the record," said the Sergeant. "We'll need a statement in the next few days, once you've got things sorted out. Is there somewhere we can reach you?"
"You can always try the shop," said I.

After a brief exchange of identities, I rejoined the Professor and we entered the flat. The hall was a mess, the Professor's worldly goods all charred and soggy.

"Are you insured?" said the Professor.
"Yes, I think so," said I.
"What do you mean, 'You think so'?" said the Professor. "Either you are or you aren't."

"House insurance was a condition of the mortgage," said I, "but I've no idea what contents insurance there is."

"Well that's just great!" said the Professor, bitterly.

We inspected the rest of the flat. All the doors were shut but every room stank of smoke.

"I can't face this just now," said I.
"Where to then?" said the Professor.
"Couldn't we stay at your house?" said I. "It is an emergency."
"Well, she always had a soft spot for you," said the Professor, "but I don't fancy my chances much."
"It's worth a try," said I.

I locked up. We got into the Professor's car and drove in silence over to the Grange.

The Professor stopped outside his recent home.

"In you go then," said the Professor.
"Aren't you coming?" said I.
"I think not," said the Professor.

I walked up the gravel drive and rang the door bell. Footsteps on the stairs, porch lantern lit and the outer door opened.

"Hello!" said I.
"Hello stranger!" said Julia. "What brings you here? Has that miserable bugger sent you round to plead for him?"
"Not exactly," said I. "Can I come in?"
"Of course!" said Julia. "How can I help?"

Julia and I have always been fond of each other. Too fond. We stood in the hall.

"So what's up?" said Julia.

Repetition becomes tiresome.

"... so we're both temporarily homeless," said I.
"You know you're always welcome," said Julia, "but there's no way he's staying here. Maybe he could sleep in the greenhouse. That would be fitting."

Accept? Protest? Temporise? Argue? I said nothing. Of course he'd behaved appallingly.

"Piggy in the middle?" said Julia sardonically. "Anyway, what about the cottage? It's only an hour away."
"Good thinking!" said I.
"I'll find you a key," said Julia. "There's bedding up there."

She rootled in the top left drawer of the hall chest and handed me a large mortise key.

"I don't know why you put up with him," said Julia. "He uses you something rotten. Just like everyone else."
"You used to say there was something good in everyone," said I.
"Not much in his case," said Julia, opening the front door.

I turned to go but she reached out and took my arm.

"Do you think I'm over-reacting?" said Julia.
"No," said I. "Not at all. But he is my friend and he's always stood by me."

"Bloody male bonding," said Julia. "You'll be stripping off and banging drums on Cramond Beach next."

"We did that years ago," said I. "Weren't you there as well? Dressed in cheesecloth and crushed velvet?"

"Don't remind me," said Julia. "Anyway, I hope you can get your place cleaned up soon."

"Thanks again," said I.

"Have a nice holiday!" said Julia, shutting the door behind me.

The car was gone. I trudged back up Lauder Road to the flat and put some relatively untainted socks and underpants into the bag, along with Napier's notes, the *Green Child* and the contents of the fridge.

Must eat. Now. A bowl of tomato soup and a cheese and ham croissant would do just fine.

Outside the flat the customer was waiting.

"We've some unfinished business," said the customer.

"We have not," said I, trying to push past him.

From behind, his companion pinioned my arms.

"We need some of your blood," said the customer. "Just a drop. It won't hurt. There's something very strange about your physiology."

"Because I'm not dead yet?" said I.

"How would you know the difference?" said the customer. "His left hand please."

The customer felt in his hold-all and took out a syringe. He then tore open a sterile packet and fitted a new needle onto the nozzle.

"The left thumb, please," said the customer. "If he struggles, break it."

The customer jabbed my thumb with the needle and squeezed. A dark ball of blood collected.

Citizens demand police!

"Hold still," said the customer, bending over me.

Now! I kneed the customer in the groin, wriggled free from his companion and fled.

Along Warrender Park Road, up Lover's Loan past the high garden walls of the huge haughty houses and over the main road at St Catherine's church. The Grange cemetery gate scraped on the gravel as I opened it.

The north wall shelters Victorian family gravestones. I walked along beside it, listening for sounds of pursuit, browsing the inscriptions: teachers and ministers, suddenly and after a long illness, soldiers and sailors, still birth and childbirth, shopkeepers and colonial administrators, influenza and whooping cough, beloved wives and mothers, in action and of wounds, aunts and sisters, professors and missionaries.

The text on the Stuarts' resting place was eroded by pollution, but the dates on the bas-relief palm tree still looked fresh. A familiar golden glow from the right side of the panel. The cemetery gate opened: footfall on gravel. I pulled the panel forward and stepped into the lift. The panel shut behind me.

Two buttons: up and down. I pushed down and descended sedately. The vestibule at the bottom held a telephone. A familiar red light blinked on the hand piece. I picked it up.

"Thank you for choosing Timeline," said the androgynous mid-Atlantic voice. "When instructed, select one to reverse time; select two to bifurcate time; select three to freeze time. Select now, please."

I did nothing.

"You have not made a selection," said the voice. "For other services please insert a credit card."

I frantically fossicked for the Book Token card and swiped it into the reader.

"To travel, select one…" said the voice.

I pushed:

   1

"Please enter your destination code," said the voice.

Destination code? The six numbers in the file? 'Geneva' and 'Grange' both have six letters?

Each digit on the key pad had three letters associated with it. Desperately, I punched in:

   814484

"You have selected Tahiti," said the voice. "Please travel now."

I opened the exit and stepped through.

6. Sur la plage

Darkness. Warmth. A smell of overripe fruit. Throbbing noise. Rolling motion. I felt in my pocket, found the book of matches and struck one. The small rectangular metal space was full of boxes of papaya. I swayed down the central aisle, pushed on the door and emerged into a moonlit loading bay. Up the steel ladder and onto the deck.

The Southern Cross. Fractured peaks silhouetted against the sky. Orion upside down on the horizon. I turned to face the bows. We were fast approaching a harbour: to the right, a town strung out along the strand.

Back to the boxes. Wet sticky floor: I squat by the door, I don't know how long for.

This is all rather unlikely. Ten thousand kilometres from the customer, from Napier's bones and epiphany machines. But Tahiti, for gods' sakes! How to stay alive? How to get home? How to get off this ship? Jump overboard? Sharks? Currents? Give myself up? How would French hospitality compare with Swiss? Ou ete le consul Britannique? Ecosses? Time to eat.

I felt in the bag and found: the end of a loaf of brown bread; a jar of peanut butter; a half litre carton of full cream milk; a tub of Soya margarine. With the large blade on the Scotch army knife, I carved off two slices of bread and buttered both with margarine.

Need buttering involve butter? When one butters someone up, what lubricant is applied? Orgy butter?

I spread one slice thickly with peanut butter, sandwiched it up and wolfed it down.

The boat lurched and came to a slow stop. The diesel engine died. Footsteps on the gang plank. Then quiet. Replete, I left the hold and went back up on deck. We were berthed at the far end of the harbour. No one around. I stepped onto dry land.

Drums of oil, bales of barbed wire, stacks of hardwood, sacks of cement, pallets of copra and pineapple. Two emaciated Polynesians shooting up in the shadows. A party of animated American tourists disembarking from a cruise ship. Disney's finest. I tagged along behind.

Warm. Half moon. Eyelid of god. Waxing or waning? Yes, of course there were palm trees.

Out of the harbour onto the boulevard. The Tourist Office was shut. As was the bank. I checked the exchange rates display: *100 CFP <=> 0.48 pound*. Along the boulevard: boutique, cafe, hotel, water sports, trinkets, boutique, cafe, hotel, water sports, trinkets. Browse the windows, dividing by two hundred: French culture; French prices. Left up a side street and right onto the rue: boutique, cafe, hotel, water sports, trinkets, boutique, ...

... *Le Pub Anglais*. Union Jack over the door. Bureau de change sign in the window. I went in. On the walls, photos of Somerset Maugham, Rupert Brooke and Robert Louis Stevenson. Yes, of course he was Scots. I approached the barman.

"Do you speak English?" said I.
"Too bloody right mate," said the barman, in a pronounced Eastern European accent.
"What time is it, please?" said I.

The barman pointed to the brass model of Big Ben on the spirits shelf. Synecdoche.

Ten o'clock. Something wrong somewhere. It must have been around eight p.m. when I left Edinburgh. I'd lost four hours from Geneva to Edinburgh. Maybe it takes four hours no matter what the distance is? Tahiti's around ten hours behind Scotland. Maybe it should be two p.m. here? How long was I in the hold? But it was dark when I got here?

"Is the clock right?" said I.
"Stopped years ago," said the barman. "What you drinking?"
"What English beer do you have, please?" said I.
"Guinness, Tooheys and Budweiser," said the barman.
"How much?" said I.

The barman named an unimaginably large sum.

"I think not," said I.

The barman smiled.

"On the house!" said the barman. "You're my first customer this morning!"

The barman opened a can of Guinness and passed it to me.

"Cheers mate!" said I, taking a long pull.

Flat. Metallic. Warm.

"Haven't seen you before, mate," said the barman. "Been here long?"
"Not very," said I. "And you?"
"Twenty three years," said the barman. "Bloody marvellous place. Bloody marvellous people."
"Where are you from?" said I.
"Poland," said the barman. "Where you from?"
"Scotland," said I.
"Used to be lots of people from Scotland here," said the barman. "Tried to grow cotton. All dead now."
"What were they called?" said I.
"Stewart," said the barman.

Felix is called Stuart. The grave stone in the Grange was for the Stuarts. The martyrs' monument has a plaque of John Knox preaching to Mary Queen of Scots, a Stewart. There are no coincidences.

"Where did they live?" said I.
"Atimaono," said the barman. "There's a golf course there now."
"Where are they buried?" said I.
"No bloody clue mate," said the barman.
"How do I get there?" said I.
"Where?" said the barman.
"Atimaono!" said I.
"Get *le truck* west to Faaa," said the barman. "From the market. Left out of here and you can't miss it."
"Can I change some money?" said I.
"That's what the bloody sign says," said the barman.

I handed over a twenty five pound note.

"What's this?" said the barman.

"Twenty five pounds," said I.

"Where's it from?" said the barman.

"Scotland!" said I.

"Never seen one of these before," said the barman.

"The Scots pound's worth about three percent less than the English pound," said I.

"Right mate!" said the barman, taking the note, inspecting it, tapping at the till and returning an insultingly small quantity of CFP.

"Come on!" said I. "What rates are you using? Surely there should be more than this."

"It's all the commission," said the barman. "Take it or bloody leave it."

It was still dark outside. I walked back along the rue to the market and found the stand for Faaa. *Le truck* was once a flat-bed lorry. The cabin on the back had wooden benches along both sides. I asked the driver for Atimaono: he wordlessly took my handful of notes. I climbed aboard and perched on the end of the near side bench.

No shy sarong smiles: sleepy commuter taciturnity; baseball caps, blue jeans, trainers and T shirts; irritatingly unidentifiable tsh-ata-tsh-ata-tshing from personal stereos. It could have been the 45 to Riccarton.

Le truck stopped at Faaa airport. My fellow passengers all got off.

"Give us a hand," said the solitary woman, passing up a bulging rucksack.

I put it on the floor between the benches.

"God, I hate that flight from Los Angeles," said the woman, sitting down opposite me as *le truck* set off.

Long raven tresses down diaphanous robes. Totally bald beneath rainbow skull cap. Blonde curls escaping from sou'wester sides. Does it really matter what she looked like? Stout walking boots and denim jump suit off set by a delicate necklace of cowrie shells. Yes, short brown hair and steel rimmed glasses.

I said nothing. *Le truck* rattled along the road.

"So why are you here?" said the woman as we crossed a bridge.
"Simple twist of fate," said I.
"Idiot wind?" said the woman.

Repetition becomes tiresome.

"... as I was going to be in this part of the world anyway, I thought I'd see if there was any truth in the old family stories," said I.
"If you're looking for Scotch gravestones," said the woman, "the nearest place to your great great grandfather's plantation must be the Protestant Church in Papara."
"That certainly sounds promising," said I. "Our family's always been Presbyterian. Would you tell me when we're near, please?"
"Sure," said the woman. "It's this side of Atimaono. I'll ask the driver to stop there."

She banged on the cab's rear window and shouted in French.

"You seem to know this area well," said I.
"I should do," said the woman. "I've been back every summer for the last 6 years"
"So what brings you here?" said I.
"CNEXO," said the woman. "They breed shrimps. I'm checking how they adjust to radioactivity."

"Why here?" said I.

"Where have you been?" said the woman. "This is where the French test their bombs."

"But that's hundreds of kilometres away," said I. "Anyway, there haven't been any tests for ages."

"So how come radiation levels in crustacean exoskeletons are so much higher here than anywhere else in the South Pacific?" said the woman brittley.

I said nothing. *Le truck* crossed a second bridge.

"I'm sorry," said the woman. "I'm really short of sleep."

"Never apologise, never explain," said I.

"I just thought that someone Scotch would know about these things," said the woman, "especially after what Torness did to all the North Sea sand eels."

"Didn't they say it was the seals?" said I.

"That's what they said at first," said the woman, "but it turned out to be low level waste leaks from the on-site cooling ponds."

"You're very well informed," said I.

"I need to be," said the woman. "It's my life's work. Reading Karen Silkwood's biography at school was a real epiphany for me."

That word.

"Napier's bones," said I softly.

The woman grabbed her rucksack and moved quickly over to the farthest corner.

"Stay away from me!" she screamed. "I should have guessed!"

Le truck shuddered to a halt. I opened the rear door and leapt out. *Le truck* drew off into the dawn.

There are no conspiracies? Or coincidences?

The churchyard was surrounded by low whitewashed walls. I followed the central path to the church and walked round the outside. At the rear, a large ornamental urn, bluebells carved on the plinth, "Stewart" on the plaque. I climbed up and bent over the urn. Nothing. I walked round the plinth, looking for signs of movement. Nothing. I tried to rock the urn but it was set solid.

Scorpions? Snakes? Spiders? I reached in to the urn and felt for a catch.

The plinth swivelled about the front left corner. Escalator descending through golden light. I got on. The plinth closed above me. At the bottom, in the conservatory, the phone.

Where to go to? How to get there? Are all codes 6 letters? Was "Tahiti" a coincidence? Felix would know. "Geneva" has 6 letters.

I picked up the hand set - RBT - swiped the card, typed in:

436382

opened the French windows and stepped through...

...into my room in the Cornavin, the half empty bottle of Scotch on the bedside table. I checked the bag and took out the three quarters empty bottle.

I haven't travelled in time. But if the bottle's here then I'm still having supper with Felix.

The startled doorman let me out. I crossed the road and ran back through the station underpass to the pedestrian precinct. It was warm and my clothes felt tight. From the shadows of the bench opposite, I could just see myself and Felix at the rear of the coffee bar.

Paradoxes make my brains buzz. I hadn't met myself before. So what would happen now if I did go in and join them? Is there a club for diners who don't dine with themselves? Bearded barbers don't shave.

I waited until I left the cafe. Shortly afterwards Felix emerged and disappeared through the door to the apartments upstairs. After a decent interval, I crossed the precinct and rang the bell for 'Haddock'.

I do seem to spend a lot of time applying verbs to electro-mechanical interfaces.

The bolt unshot and I walked up the stairs round the central lift shaft. The first door on the first floor was open. I went in, shutting it behind me. The hall was unlit but from a door to the right the 'Art of Fugue' braided golden. I opened it and went in.

"I thought you'd come," said Felix from the armchair. "I knew I wouldn't have to wait long."

He turned towards me.

"Ah," he said, after a short pause. "You've been travelling."
"How can you tell?" said I, sitting down in the armchair on the other side of the fireplace.
"You've changed," said Felix. "Haven't you noticed?"

I felt my chin.

"Not the beard," said Felix. "You're slightly thicker all over, as if you were four months pregnant. Without the bump."

I looked him up and down.

"Precisely," said Felix.
"How many journeys?" said I.
"I lost count," said Felix.
"Is it irreversible?" said I.
"It depends what you mean," said Felix. "It is for these instances of us. So far."
"Why didn't you tell me?" said I.
"It wouldn't have made any difference." said Felix.
"Of course it would!" said I. "I might have behaved differently!"
"Then you wouldn't have been this instance of you, would you," said Felix.
"So I can't have told you."
"Would it make any difference if I tell you what happens next?" said I.
"Do you know if you did?" said Felix.
"How?" said I.
"From what happens when what happens next happens!" said Felix.

I put my head in my hands.

"Don't worry," said Felix. "I still think you're stunning."

Ignore him.

"So when you see me next you'll know what's going to happen to me but you won't tell me?" said I.
"Do I tell you?" said Felix.
"No," said I.

"Then I won't tell this you," said Felix. "I might tell another you. But then it won't be this me that tells that other you."

"This makes little sense," said I.

"Have a drink," said Felix.

He got up, opened the cocktail cabinet, took out a bottle of Armagnac and poured two large shots into crystal glasses.

"Popular ideas about time and space are all crap," said Felix. "Just look at science fiction. Wells' traveller zips up and down a one dimensional time stream. Vonnegut's Trafalmadoreans exist simultaneously throughout unchanging linear personal histories. For Lem, time is a strange loop where paradox accumulates until resolved through his hero's sheer strength of character. Zelazney's Shadow is a multi-dimensional hallucinogenic walking tour, traversed by unchanging individuals' acts of will. Moorcock's Multiverse starts off as a tangle of Wellsian time streams and becomes probabilistically post-modern. Individuals change but retain core essences like Hindu avatars."

"So you've read lots of cheap paperbacks," said I. "I'm impressed."

"Reality's much simpler," said Felix, ignoring me. "The universe contains a finite amount of matter which can be in a finite number of states. According to the many worlds interpretation, all those states exist simultaneously as superimposed possibilities. What we experience as linear changes in time and space is just movement from state to state. Normally, the difference between successive states is very very small so moving from one to another takes tiny amounts of energy."

"When you say that all states exist simultaneously, you mean all possible states?" said I.

"Any state that doesn't flaunt the laws of physics," said Felix.

"Even states where there are concurrent versions of me?" said I.

"Is that physically impossible?" said Felix. "There's an astonishing quantity of matter in the universe, easily enough for a galaxy of variants of you, all slightly different."

"This makes less sense," said I.

"Look," said Felix. "You've read Borges. In the Library of Babel, there's a finite number of finite sized books, containing all possible permutations of a finite number of letters. You can find millions of versions of the same story, all slightly different. Dennet suggests that they could be held in a multi-dimensional shelving system where each book has only one letter different to the one next to it. If you selected books in turn, eventually you'd find a chain linking any two books together. But the bigger the difference between the books, the more other books you'd have to read to get from the first to the last."

"I can't take all this in," said I.

"It's like those puzzles," said Felix. "Change 'cat' to 'dog' in four moves."

"Cat, cot, cog, dog," said I.

"Right," said Felix. "You changed one letter each time. Now change 'crocodile' to 'alligator'. But to make it easier you don't have to make a real word every time."

"There are nine letters, so it'll take nine changes," said I.

"Good," said Felix. "Most of the books in the Library of Babel are gibberish but by picking the right sequence of changes you can always move between arbitrary sensible books. Of course there are lots of different sequences linking any two books. Actually, there's an infinite number if you're allowed to go through the same book again and again. Also, if you weren't careful you might think you'd reached the last book when in fact you'd found a subtle variant."

"'Reader, I buried him'," said I.

"Precisely," said Felix. "The old ones are the best."

"So how does Timeline work?" said I.

"It finds a state satisfying where you want to be with the least difference to the state you're in," said Felix. "It then generates enough energy for the superimposed states to collapse into that state."

"So why aren't I here three days from now?" said I.

"Look," said Felix. "The number of possible states is fabulously huge. It can't possibly search all the paths from the current one. It just finds the first state that meets some criteria of acceptability."

"How long does that take?" said I.

"Millions of years, usually," said Felix, "but it hardly matters once you've made the change."

"So where was I all that time?" said I.

"Now there's a category mistake," said Felix.

"So it didn't actually take four hours to get me from here to Edinburgh?" said I.

"When?" said Felix. "Oh never mind. If the state it found for you was more or less exact apart from a four hour difference then you did quite well. Where have you just come from?"

"Tahiti," said I.

"When?" said Felix.

"It was early morning," said I, "but I've no idea what the date was."

"They'll tell you in your monthly statement," said Felix. "They itemise all the trips."

"But I'm not registered with them," said I.

"You don't need to register," said Felix, "so long as you've got credit."

"Is it expensive?" said I.

"Depends how much and how far you travel," said Felix. "Anyway, how did you work out where to find the booths?"

RBT.

"… especially when I heard that there were Scots there called Stewart." said I.

"Total coincidence!" said Felix.

"So it isn't a Scottish connection?" said I.

"Says who?" said Felix.

Tired and weary.

"Can you get me home?" said I.
"I can," said Felix, "but are you sure you want to?"
"Yes!" said I.
"But think of the fun we could have here!" said Felix. "Anyway, another trip will play hell with your figure."
"Isn't a state where I'm thinner equally probable?" said I.

Felix surveyed his imposing bulk and looked back at me.

"No," said Felix. "It isn't."

Wired and teary.

"Can you put me up for the night?" said I.
"Oh joy!" said Felix.
"The floor would do just fine," said I.
"Have the sofa," said Felix. "I'll find you some bedding."

I took off my coat and followed Felix into the hall.

"You look like you need to freshen up," said Felix, indicating one of several identical doors. "There are spare towels in the cupboard."

I turned on the switch by the door and went into the bathroom. Every surface was mirrored. Soft light from the corners of the room cast no shadows. The door shut seamlessly and I was momentarily lost in an infinity of myself. I recalled the Charles Adams cartoon of the man peering into opposing mirrors: several levels down a hideous face leers back.

I undressed and put my clothes on the mirrored bench by the door. The shower rose came straight out of the ceiling on the far side. No soap or shampoo. I carefully studied the far wall and noticed the faint outline of a panel. At my touch it swivelled open revealing a shelf of tiny bottles and packets from miscellaneous hotels. I selected Taj Intercontinental shampoo and conditioner, and a bar of Luxor unscented ivory. The shower was controlled by chromium plated taps, nearly flush with the wall. I adjusted the flow and temperature, and stepped into the spray. Water ran back across the gently concave floor to the central drain.

It's somewhat unnerving being able to see all over at once. I hurriedly soaped myself, washed my hair and rinsed off, all the while watching unfamiliar muscle movements in a myriad of unlikely profiles.

Hunt the cupboard. Once again I inspected the walls, pushing at plausible positions. A new door to the left of the entrance opened away from me. In the bedroom beyond lay Felix, bulbous also tapered, entwined in unidentifiable limbs.

"Care to join us?" said Felix, looking up.
"Thank you but no," said I, hastily.
"Try the other side," said Felix, returning his attention to his partner.

I shut the door, located the cupboard, dried myself with a large white Kalahari Sands towel, put my clothes back on and returned to Felix's bedroom.

Felix sat cross legged on the bed, dressed in red and white striped pyjamas, smoking a cigar, alone.

"I'm sorry," said I. "This is all too much for me."
"I left England to get away from people like you," said Felix.
"So did I," said I.

"It didn't do you much good," said Felix.
"Look," said I, "I'm not homophobic."
"What makes you think I'm gay?" said Felix.
"Are you bisexual?" said I.
"Who needs all these labels?" said Felix. "I'm totally undiscriminating. I like sex and it's better with other people."

Change the subject. Politely.

"Any chance of a bite to eat?" said I.
"But we've just had supper," said Felix.
"I suppose I can't be hungry then," said I.
"Of course you can!" said Felix. "I'm forgetting my hostly duties. There's some fruit in the drawing room. Help yourself and do get some sleep, there's a good chap."
"Thanks," said I.
"Before you go," said Felix, "what's the difference between a licensed gun owner and a monastery on reclaimed land?"
"No idea," said I, patiently.
"One's a permit holder and the other's a hermit polder," said Felix.
"Thundering typhoons!" said I.
"In a blue blistering barnacle!" said Felix. "Good night!"

7. In transit

The bowl was piled high but I'd seen enough tropical fruit for one day. I got undressed. The sleeping bag smelt of warm damp cat. The sofa was soft and firm but I slept fitfully nonetheless. Little plot and less sign of closure. Racing brain, round and round.

I'm back in Geneva and it's now Saturday morning so I'm also about to wake up in the Cornavin and go and meet Felix in his shop. I've a return flight to Edinburgh and a Scots passport valid from tomorrow. I could always go back and rescue myself so I needn't go to Tahiti but then I wouldn't be here so I couldn't go back and rescue myself. But I didn't, did I. No justified sinner I.

When the birds started singing I got up and followed the smell of bacon to the kitchen. The woman, her back to me, was bent over the frying pan.

"Do you want some breakfast?" said she, without turning round.
"That'd be nice, thank you," said I. "Can I do anything?"
"The kettle's just boiled," said she, "and the coffee's in the cupboard over the work surface."
"How many cups?" said I.
"Two if you want some," said she.
"What about Felix?" said I.
"He's just gone to the shop," said she. "He's expecting someone from the UK."

"That'll be me," I said.
"But you're here," said she. "That makes no sense. Do you want any toast?"

Not a conspirator then. Or a consummately good one.

"Yes please," said I, putting three scoops of coffee from the Majolica jar into the cafetière.
"There's brown and white in the fridge," said she.
"Right," said I. "Do you want some?"
"Two brown, please," said she.

I took out four slices, pushed them into the pop up toaster and filled the cafetière from the automatic cordless kettle.

"There are plates and coffee bowls above the sink," said she. "The cutlery's in the drawer."

I laid the table. The toast popped up. I put two slices on each plate. She put two rashers on each slice. I poured the coffee. We sat down facing each other.

Discreet charm.

"I'm sorry to impose on you like this," said I.
"That's fine," said she. "It happens all the time. Felix collects waifs and strays."

Am I an abandoned pet?

"He's been very generous," said I, guardedly, "but he seems a wee bit intemperate."
"Don't mind Felix," said she. "He means well but he's not really a people person."

Is this the same Felix I met before I started travelling?

"Have you known him long?" said I.
"We'll've been married twenty five years next month," said she.

Does it make any difference?

We finished the meal in silence.

"Shall I wash up?" said I.
"The machine's under the sink," said she.
"I've never used one before," said I.
"The front folds down," said she. "Just slot everything in. I'll do the rest."

I cleared the table.

"Where are you from?" said she.
"Edinburgh," said I.
"Oh, I just love Edinburgh!" said she. "There's such a range of shops, especially for whole food and alternative medicine. Do you know Napier's the Herbalists on Bristo Place?"

Go on. Give it a try.

"Napier's bones," said I, softly.
"Has it shut then?" said she. "That's a shame. They used to have a great range of homeopathic remedies. Is that wonderful vegetarian restaurant on Hanover Street still going?"
"Hendersons?" said I. "I think so. But you eat meat?"
"That was textured soya protein," said she. "Couldn't you tell?"
"It's very convincing," said I. "But why eat something which pretends to be

meat if you're vegetarian?"

"I really miss bacon," said she, wistfully. "And sausages. Anyway, I better get going."

"So what do you do?" said I.

"I'm a counsellor," said she.

"Non directive?" said I.

She looked baffled.

"No one would vote for me if I was non directive," said she.

"Elective therapy?" said I, equally confused.

"Ah," said she. "No. I'm on the National Council."

"Right," said I.

"Will you be here this evening?" said she, getting up.

"I've a flight home this afternoon," said I.

"See you around then," said she.

"Indeed," said I. "Felix knows how to contact me. Do get in touch if you're ever in Edinburgh. And thanks for breakfast."

"It was nice to meet you," said she. "I'm so sorry you couldn't join us last night."

I followed her to the hall. She let herself out. Did I check behind each door? I did not. I went back to the drawing room and picked up my coat and bag. By the sofa was a copy of last year's *Timeline User Guide* and a note:

> *Help yourself! See you earlier? F.I.S.H.*

I browsed the first few pages of the manual, *<see Appendix 2>*, in a desultory fashion; clearly Felix's primary source. I put the book in the bag and left the flat. Walking along the precinct towards the Lake, I felt through my jacket pockets. Still lots of Swiss francs left. I turned left to the bus station and checked the timetable. Five minutes later I was on the bus, crossing the city, heading south east for Annemasse.

We kissed yesterday and she's dead in the next twenty-four hours. Or not. So maybe she's still alive today.

The bus dropped me in the square. I walked back to her apartment.

On the grass, the man arranged six biscuits in endless sequences. Beside a tree, his dog marked its territory. On the bench, the woman wrote in her notebook, sun glancing golden off the cover. By the pond, the small boy beat a metal drum.

I engaged with the entry phone. After a long pause, her voice from the grille:

"Who is it?"
"It's me," said I.

Another long pause.

"You better come up then."

She met me on the landing, sweating profusely, goose pimple shivered.

"Are you alone?" said I, looking round.
"For the moment," said she. "What do you want?"
"You don't look too well," said I.
"The coward does it with a kiss," said she.
"Who's the coward?" said I. "You or me?"
"You could never face up to anything," said she. "Get on with it then. I haven't got all day."
"But I'm not dead," said I.

"Not yet," said she.

"Not like the man in the shop," said I. "How many others?"

"Too many," said she.

"Napier's bones?" said I.

"Sod off!" said she. "I've nothing to tell you."

"What about the epiphany machine," said I.

"So what's an epiphany?" said she.

"Three wise men," said I.

"That'll be the day," said she.

"The old ones are the best," said I. "Twelfth Night."

"Look," said she, "you know what an orgasm is."

"Indeed I do," said I.

"There was never any doubt about that," said she.

"Do go on," said I.

"You know what a peak experience is?" said she.

"Divine revelation," said I. "Induced by trance or drugs or fasting or sleep deprivation."

"Orgasm and peak experiences are extremes," said she. "Maximum stimulation of the pleasure centres. One knocks your socks off. The other makes you suddenly aware that you're not wearing them."

She hugged herself.

"I'm freezing," said she. "I'm going to put the fire on."

We went through to the sitting room: nondescript rented furniture; white leather upholstered suite; white melamine bookcase, bare; TV.

She lit the fire.

"An epiphany's when you have a momentary almost intuitive understanding," said she. "Originally it meant a cosmic manifestation, just like a peak experience, but now it's softened. It's sometimes used to mean a sudden self realisation brought on by something relatively ordinary."

"More of an 'Aha!' experience?" said I.

"You're still into pop psychology then," said she. "Much more intense."

"Are they nice," said I.

"Oh yes," said she. "You've probably never had one."

"Addictive?" said I.

"They would be," said she. "if you could find some way of generating them. That's the problem. You don't know you're going to have one 'til you've had it."

"So an epiphany machine's a machine that stimulates epiphanies?" said I.

"Well done!" said she.

Napier's bones. Well, if not the bones then maybe the ligaments?

"Does anyone know how to build one?" said I.

"Oh yes," said she.

"Have you tried it?" said I.

"Oh yes," said she.

Pause for thought.

"Not so nice then?" said I.

"No," said she. "They weren't all my epiphanies."

"What happened?" said I.

"I thought it was just another job," said she. "I went along to the test centre and they said they'd a new home entertainment system for evaluation. I thought it would just be another third rate game but it was quite different. Somehow they can evoke really deep memories, a bit like that bloke who could get patients to recall random life events during brain surgery through electrical stimulation. Only this didn't involve any physical intervention. Anyway, to begin with I was remembering really nice things from when I was wee, things I'd never really forgotten but hadn't thought about for ages, things which in retrospect were truly defining moments, in amazing detail."

"What sort of things?" said I.

"Oh, the first one was finding out that I could actually stay upright on a bicycle under my own steam," said she. "My dad had tried to teach me to ride on his bike but it was far too big and I was terrified of falling over. Anyway, one day he lost patience and just let me go. Suddenly I was peddling and steering and staying upright all at the same time. It felt astonishingly good, that realisation of control and the knowledge that I could do it whenever I wanted to. It was incredibly vivid. I really was there all over again. I could see him and sense his frustration and feel my desire to please him and my fear of failing and the steady build up of terror of losing balance and then the sudden resolution and relief and self assurance. I must have been seven or so. I could see the street and the road and the trees and the sky and the houses as if it had happened exactly the same all over again."

"Sounds really good!" said I.

"There were several like that," said she, "but then it began to change. The memories were just as vivid but somehow not quite right. I felt a curious fascination to stay with it to see what would happen next but there was also a growing disquiet that what I was experiencing hadn't actually happened to me. The memories became less and less my own, and more and more extreme. But the voyeurism was very, very strong, like watching an unpleasant film where you're torn between walking out and staying to see how things develop. Eventually it all became too much and I stopped but by then it was too late. The later experiences were unspeakably unpleasant but ever since there's been this deep nagging sense that they might have been true memories and I'd somehow forgotten them. They're incredibly intense and leave this obsessive need to try them again to work out why they're so wrong but so persuasive. The whole thing's extraordinarily manipulative."

"What sort of experiences?" said I.

She looked at me, pointedly.

"What's all this got to do with me?" said I.

"You stupid bastard!" said she. "You're the key!"

"To what?" said I.

"To destroying it!" said she.

"You want to destroy the epiphany machine?" said I.

"Sharp as ever," said she.

"But I don't understand," said I.

"He told you!" said she. "You're carrying a virus."

Dumb show.

"My cold?" said I.

"It's not just a cold!" said she. "It kills everyone that catches it, apart from you. Needs contact to pass it on."

"The dead bloke's hanky?" said I. "Handling it was enough to infect me?"

"Looks like it," said she. "And it isn't stable long enough for us to decode it."

"What's encoded?" said I.

"The root password for the epiphany machine," said she. "We need it so we can shut it down."

So what were the numbers in the file then?

"Why didn't you just tell me?" said I.

"My knight in shining armour?" said she. "You could barely look after yourself. Is Robin still tidying up after you?"

"Why are you so angry with me?" said I.

She looked at me, sullenly.

"You know just fine!" said she.

The psychic wheels turned slowly.

"But that was so long ago," said I. "I thought we'd put that behind us."
"You thought!" said she.
"This is crazy!" said I. "Why has this come up now?"
"There's no point in going over it again," said she. "Life's too short. Just go away."

Do I lack solicitude? Do I gloat at her ill fortune? Am I its guilty vector?

"But you need help," said I, lamely.
"From you?" said she. "Don't make me laugh. At least I knew what I was doing. What are you going to do? Join a monastery?"
"What do you mean?" said I
"You're a fucking disaster area," said she. "Talk about Typhoid Mario! I don't much fancy your chances for long term relationships."
"Is there an antidote?" said I.
"Not yet," said she.
"Who developed it?" said I.
"The Grassmarket Institute," said she. "Ironic eh?"
"Maybe the Professor would know someone there," said I.
"Maybe," said she.
"Maybe they could help you?" said I.
"It's a wee bit late for that," said she.

How did we part? Did I cradle her in my arms? I did not. Did we hug brief regrets? We did not. Hugging is totally un-British. For Brits, any physical contact apart from shaking hands is redolent of sex. Even the tepid hug, where the hugees pat each other's backs to avoid sustained contact, is fraught with ambiguity.

On the stairs, did I pass the express delivery bearing the cure I'd sent to her next week? I did not. Don't I care? Of course I care! But what can I do? If she doesn't die then I don't need to do anything and if she does die then it hardly matters how long it takes me to ensure that she doesn't. Maybe contingency has something to recommend it?

Bus to the bus station; train to the airport; sit by the entrance waiting for myself to be driven away and for the frontier guard shift to change. This time they didn't even look at my Scottish passport.

The incoming flight was regrettably delayed every twenty minutes for the next three hours. I wandered the bookshop, the duty free shop, the chocolate shop, the newsagent; paced up and down past the plate glass windows, watching the planes come in over the Jura; sat in the coffee lounge drinking stewed Ceylon. Not in any particular hurry to go anywhere, just don't want to be here very much longer.

As we finally boarded, they gave us compensatory food dispenser tokens. When we reached our cruising altitude, I joined the queue in the aisle.

"I sure miss those pretty little hostesses," said the man in front.

The machine was full of sandwiches: stale sliced crustless white bread; luncheon meat and processed cheese; margarine; cardboard and cellophane boxes. I settled for a gin and tonic in a small waxed carton from the drinks bank.

Level flight. Unbroken cloud below. I leant back, sucked at the straw and dipped into the in-flight magazine:

SWEET OR SAVOURY?

Did you know that your food preferences can tell you a surprising amount about what sort of person you are? Psychologists have discovered that almost everyone has either a sweet or a savoury personality. And this affects how they get on with other people. Try our tasteful quiz to find out which sort you are!

Would you rather:

1) buy
i) a hot dog or
ii) an ice cream
at the cinema?

2) sprinkle
i) salt or
ii) sugar
on your porridge?

3) serve
i) tomato ketchup or
ii) pineapple
with gammon steak?

4) nibble
i) celery or
ii) carrot
sticks between meals?

5) drink
i) Bloody Mary or
ii) whisky and cola
at a cocktail party?

6) spread
i) dripping or
ii) marmalade
on toast?

If your answers are mostly i)s then you're a "savoury" type and if they're mostly ii)s then you're a "sweet". So what does this say about you? You might expect a sweet person to be straightforward and good natured while a savoury person might be a bit more complex and moody. Perhaps women tend to be sweet while men are more savoury? Of course, things are more complicated than this. Sugar and salt are both vital for life but both are addictive and, in excess, can be positively harmful. What's best is a moderate balance. So too with the human personality...

Pah! Abject drivel!

I slipped the limp rag back between the fish net and the safety card, and reached beneath the seat in front for my bag...

...He had acquired that final wisdom, which sees in the soul a disturber of the peace of the body. The soul it is that incites the senses to seek spiritual satisfaction. But the only satisfactions are physical, measured and immutable...

Read's materialism, trench spawned, was neither dialectical nor mechanical:

...Wars are occasioned by the love of power and power has to be acquired by force to satisfy the demands of spiritual pride... Experience has proved to me, that if we would have pure knowledge of anything we must be quit of the soul - the body in itself must achieve a state of harmony and perfection...

I've read *The Green Child* so often that I almost know it by heart, but I still find it strangely comforting:

...And thus having got rid of the fluctuations of the spirit, we shall be pure and become part of the universal harmony, and know in ourselves the law of the physical universe, which is no other than the law of truth...

As we began our descent, the ghost in the machine kicked back in. Ghost of electricity. Through the cloud, we were over the Grampians, not the Lammermuirs.

The first officer apologised profusely, the landing at Aberdeen was smooth and a bus was waiting for us. An hour or so later I was dropped on the Dundee ring road. No point in going back home: I'd the keys to the Professor's cottage and two days to kill.

I walked down the hill, through the city to the Tay Bridge, and stuck out a thumb on the slip road. No need for interview technique: the elderly van driver seemed glad of company. I helped decant bundles of the *Courier* at every village shop on route to St Andrews. In the 'Whey Pat', she bought me a pint of Pale Ale and a mutton pie: there's something deeply disturbing about sheep fat coagulating between the fingers but I was ravenous. Replete, the driver and I parted firm friends; she heading home to Dundee while I set off on foot for Tullybothy.

The sun was low as I walked through the West Port onto South Street. At The *Inn on the Quad*, tartan tammys fled *Golf Heritage* coaches.

The town has really gone down hill since independence day. Neraly seven hundred years ago, the University boasted one of the first Vatican franchise in these fair isles: today English local authorities won't pay maintenance grants for study at foreign institutions. Losing over seventy five percent of their income overnight, the high heidyans decamped north to rejoin the once despised Dundee, their historic patrimony now quaint hotels for the plus-fours set. Historic matrimony?

Right along the city wall, past the Byre Theatre and the Cottage Hospital and the Gatty Marine Laboratory. Up the hill beside the cliff top caravan park. At the Brownhills Garage, I stopped and turned and looked back across the city of the plain; beyond the Tay, light blue sky shot orange/red/purple.

Yes, I know this place well. It's where we all met, Robin and the Professor and she and I. Certainly a long time ago now. Clichés under the bridge.

Left onto the East Neuk road, the sharp wind from the grey North Sea rippling the green fields.

Not much traffic. Most going the wrong way. I strode on briskly. Many a time and oft I'd mopeded up and down this road, to and from the North Haugh. Little's changed. Every hill and turning still engrained on the brain, every side road and gate from which tractors might suddenly emerge. Though it all looks somewhat different at one tenth the speed.

Sore city feet soon grounded rural reverie. The Kirkcaldy bus stopped to drop passengers at the Boarhills turn off: I was in Crail within ten minutes. Left up Marketgate, past the Tollbooth and the parish church, and out of town heading north east.

Fife Ness is the craggy right angle where the Firths of Forth and Tay meet the North Sea. Tullybothy's the only beach, used variously by Danish raiders, to provision Balcomie Castle during landward sieges and by smugglers leery of the Crail excise officers. In the early nineteenth century, a model fishing village was built with stone from the abandoned fortified house. The great storm of 1818 drove the entire fleet onto Englishman's Skelly. No one survived: Tullybothy's still known locally as the village of women.

Thereafter the Wormistone Estate was the only local employer: today most of the indigenous inhabitants are ageing refugees from mechanisation. There's always a smattering of simple life white settlers but they don't usually stay past the first winter: little grows in the thin salty soil, and the East Neuk markets are stowed out with organic vegetables and batik and pottery. Thus, for much of the year the village is quiet, awaiting its suburban swallows.

The Professor's cottage abuts Mary's Skelly, at the northern end of the narrow main street that rings the beach, opposite the *Bluestane Inn* and next to the manse. I let myself in. The house smelt cold. I reached above the door and turned on the electricity. Straight across the hall into the kitchen, down with the bag and off with the coat.

Check the cupboards: tins of tomatoes and tuna and beans and soup; cellophane packets of pasta and oatmeal and lentils and dried mushrooms;

tubs of herbs and spices; a rope of garlic; a string of dried red chillies; cardboard boxes of oatcakes and matzos and chocolate biscuits; a bottle of olive oil; caddies of tea and coffee and dried milk and sugar; jars of jam and marmalade. I won't starve.

Check the fridge: two cartons of long life orange juice; a bottle of Chilean Sauvignon Blanc; a six pack of McEwans 80/-. I extracted a can, went back through the hall and turned left into the sitting room.

At first glance, the room was very different from when I'd stayed here. Children's' books and toys and rainy day board games on the shelves. Bright glossy posters from the Fisheries Museum on the walls. A pile of brochures and unwritten postcards on the coffee table.

Closer inspection revealed less change.

On the mantelpiece, sea washed stones and skeletal shells, sand smoothed glass and sun bleached wood; a mug of dried grasses and flowers; two stubby white candles in saucers.

On the top book shelf, the Professor's complete set of Biggles books, bought ostensibly for his study group's uncompleted analysis of the roots of English male attitudes; enthralling reading when abjectly stoned.

Along the wall under the seawards window, his legendary collection of 'B' LPs: Bach, Bartok, Beethoven, Berlioz, Bizet, Borodin, Bruchner, Byrd; Bessie Smith, Billie Holiday, Bird, Bix Biederbecke; B.B.King, The Beach Boys, The Beatles, Its A Beautiful Day, Captain Beefheart and His Magic Band, Big Brother and the Holding Company, Bill Haley, Blind Boy Grunt, Blind Joe Death, Bo Diddley, Bob Dylan, Bob Marley and the Wailers, The Bonzo Dog Band, The Boys of the Lough, Bridget St John, Buffy St Marie, The Byrds. Legendary?

Sitting down on the old battered sofa opposite the stone fireplace, I took a long pull at the cool, sharp beer. The window to the right looked across the street to the public bar. The window to the left looked out to sea. On the horizon, winking lights from the oil platforms. In the foreground, the North Carr Beacon swept the jagged rocks, too late for the men of Tullybothy.

The phone rang. I reached across to the table and answered it:

"Crail 327."

An unknown female voice:

"Is Eric there?"

Eric. The Professor. He'd once sported an "L" after the "E".

"I'm afraid not," said I. "Can I take a message?"
"Who are you?" said she.

I told her.

"This is Morag," said she. "He's told me a lot about you."

Not all *bad/*good I hope (*delete as appropriate). And he's told me nothing about you.

"Have you tried the lab?" said I.
"He's not there," said she.
"Have you tried email?" said I. "He's almost always on-line."
"I don't have a computer," said she.
"Have you tried his brother's?" said I.

"He's not there anymore," said she, "and they don't know where he's gone. I'm really desperate to find him. I think I'm pregnant."

Right then.

"He's staying at my flat for a while," said I, and gave her the address and phone number.
"Thanks ever so much," said she. "I began to panic when I couldn't find him anywhere. We're supposed to be getting married when his divorce comes through. Thanks again," and put the phone down.

Now there's a mistake. What if she tells him how she found him? He thinks I'm in Geneva. Aye well, needs must. Anyway, he didn't mention it when I got back from Geneva the first time...

I must stop this dubious determinism. If reality continually bifurcates then goodness knows which alternative I've just initiated. Does it matter? I'm still here and now boys, and almost certainly in Yverdon at the same time. So long as Felix gets me back home the morn and I'm in Tahiti on Monday then Hogg's loop should close and the future return to some semblance of existential normality. But if the bifurcations maintain probabilistic continuity, then what I do in the loop almost certainly does matter if I'm ever to get to the bottom of these bloody bones, slay the dragon, rescue the princess and live happily ever after. What if I'm the princess? Or the dragon?

8. In the village

I polished off the beer, went back down the hall to my old room, took fresh linen from the bottom drawer of the chest and made up the bed. This room was home for eighteen months, must be eighteen years ago now. I'm worn out. Off with the coat and shoes and stretch out, hands behind head, eyes shut?

While you here do snoring lie,/Open-ey'd conspiracy/His time doth take.

I sat on the edge of the bed and surveyed the room. Smaller than I'd remembered. Barely space for the chest and desk and wardrobe.

The wardrobe! I climbed up on the chair and felt on top. The china Balkan Sobranie box was still in the far corner. I brought it down and opened it: Rizla blue; cough sweet tin of long desiccated Golden Virginia; clay pipe; bank change bag of flowering tops. I put the box on the desk next to the computer.

A computer! And a headset. And an Outernet link.

I sat down, switched on and logged in as the Professor. We've always known each other's passwords - it doubles the number of systems we both have access to. Where to start? Cold or calculator? Blood is thicker than bone.

I clicked up the browser, surfed for the Grassmarket Institute and found the Bio-chemical Communication Group's page. Academics are not exactly publicity shy, despite all their protestations of disinterested, selfless research. At the bottom, links to recent reports and papers. How about *Survival rates in Dawkins encoded hamsters*, published earlier this year. I pulled it over into the editor and scrolled to the last page:

> ... *In summary, results from the double-blind experiments discussed above showed that a rhinovirus, which had been meme encoded through modified transfer RNA, displayed excellent transmission rates across a population through contact with saliva or sputum. However, there was a 99.5% host death rate within 3 days of rhinovirus introduction.*
>
> *While it seems reasonable to ascribe death to the rhinovirus, 4 days after its introduction it was undetectable in post-mortem analysis of all subjects, in blood, lymph or body organs. Note that, despite rigid dietary controls, above average levels of common salt were found in all the surviving subjects.*
>
> *We conclude that the relatively short life span of the rhinovirus in the host, coupled with the well known problems of subsequent meme decoding, suggest that this promising technique does not yet enable fully reliable bio-technology based communication.*

Well, it's been at least four of my days since I was infected. Monkfish no more! Saved by my savoury personality? This calls for a celebration. Another beer? A wee pipe?

Of his bones are coral made.

I logged across to the Professor's work system and opened the subdirectory containing the Australian code cracker. Near the top of the Mocha program, he'd hand coded the six bytes as hexadecimal digits. I browsed for the National Museums of Scotland home page and linked across to the Mediateque Information Service. At the Search option, I entered:

epiphany machine

Welcome to the epiphany machine.
Please enter your password:

and typed in the code:

Please select 'Start'.

I did so:

You now have 30 seconds in which to adjust your headset.

I took off my glasses, put on the headset and folded the visor down. Twin red shafts of laser light bored into my eyes and I fell forwards...

...into crisp fresh snow. I laugh and stand up. Creag Mhor. Early morning. Late spring. Looking back across Strathyre Forest to Ben Vorlich; pale mist rises from the deep green firs; quiet and still, save for the Calair Burn burbling below through Glen Buckie. Well ahead of me, she strides on up the steep slope and disappears behind the rocky crags. I struggle to catch up, fresh air raw in the nostrils, soles slipping with every step, snow caked on the boots, socks wet, toes cold, gloved hands toast warm. At the summit, the sun comes out from the behind the clouds, and she turns and smiles and I...

...fell backwards into the dingy bedroom.

Goodness me! Total recall! Utterly real! I flipped up the face plate and squinted at the screen:

Please select 'Start'.

Without pause, visor down. Once again my corneas were scanned and I fell forwards...

...onto the grass outside her residence block. It's my last day here. I really want to go up and see her but I'm not quite sure. She's been a bit offhand the last few times we've been together, as if disengaging. Early summer but late evening and a chill in the air. The sodium lamps cast long shadows as I walk round to the back of the building and look up at her window, wondering what to do. Displacement. I reach in the left hand great coat pocket, take out the tin, roll a cigarette and light it with the Zippo. Looking up again, I see her dark form against the curtain. I'm about to call out when someone else joins her. They embrace. I'm transfixed as she pulls back the curtain, opens the window, and looks out at me, and I...

...fell backwards into the chair.

But she didn't look out and see me! She'd no inkling I was there, did she? How could she have? Maybe I'd told someone else I was going round to look for her, a romantic gesture, playing for sympathy, and they warned her? Anyway, I never saw her directly, did I; just in shadow. Could she have seen me? And I didn't wear a greatcoat then, I wore a combat jacket. And I smoked Sovereign, not roll ups. If she had seen me, she never said so subsequently. This is very strange. There must be some way of running it again, a recall or replay option, not just:

Please select 'Start'.

As Popeye went over the rickety bridge, the sign always said 'You'll be sorry!'. Spinachless, I selected Start and the piercing lights pulled me forwards...

...onto the sofa. I'm so tired. The baby won't stop screaming. I haven't slept for so many nights. She's out. Not due back for a while yet. I've walked it and dandled it; I've cuddled it and talked to it; I've changed it and fed it; I've sung to it and sat still with it. I turn off the monitor and bury my ears in cushions but its cries cuts shards through me. Suddenly, I can't stand it any more. I get up, go through to our bedroom and turn the child onto its face. I return to the sitting room, curl up on the sofa and...

...fall backwards...

No. No. No. No. No. After she went out, I'd put it down on its back in the cot and dozed off on the sofa with the monitor on. The child was cold when she got home. The doctor said it had been dead for some hours. Accidental death. By asphyxiation. Must have rolled over. Right sort of age. No blame ascribed.

It had been her idea to have it. Of course I'd agreed. Of course I'd wanted it, anticipated it, cherished it, nurtured it, boasted about it, showed it off, photographed it, above all loved it. Of course I'd resented it for taking her away and yet giving her more control, for its unassailable dependence upon me, for vague promises of gratification deferred indefinitely. Could I have killed it in my sleep and forgotten about it, an act of unconscious desperation? No. No. No. No. No.

Why can't I name it? Identify its gender?

We were both ill for many months afterwards. Eventually the hurt muted, integrated. I suggested that we might have another but she didn't want to. She never blamed me, never said it was my fault, never brought it up other than in shared sorrow.

Was this what the machine showed her? No wonder she left. No wonder she wouldn't tell me. No wonder she wants to destroy it so single-mindedly. Wanted?

I removed the headset:

> *Please select 'Start'.*

and powered down the computer.

The room felt too enclosed and forbidding for sleep. I went through to the bathroom, took off my clothes, sat in the bath, put in the plug, turned on the taps and lay back as the warm water slowly swallowed me.

I must contact her. Ask her what she suspects. Tell her what I know. Is she dead? I don't have her phone number. She phoned Robin while I was away. When? Three time lines ago. I can't ask Robin before Monday evening.

The water reached the overflow. I turned off the taps with the toes.

Did they decode a blood sample before she died? If she died. They can't have done if the customer still sought my substances. Two time lines ago. Intervene or get out of the loop? Am I still in the refugee camp? Which loop am I in?

I got out of the bath, pulled out the plug, found a towel in the cupboard, dried myself and dressed.

In the kitchen, I felt in the bag for the camp directory, dialled the main number and asked for myself in slow, clear English. After a long delay, a belligerent voice informed me of my temporary, unlamented absence. I thanked her and put the phone down. And remembered the anonymous caller that sounded like me. Loop the loop. At least I'm still there. And still here. I could do with some company.

I put on my coat, locked up the cottage and crossed the road.

The Bluestane Inn is a nondescript two story sandstone mid-19th century house. The public bar runs the length of the front, the translucent window panes etched with slogans from long defunct breweries.

I pushed the swing door open and entered the deserted room. The interior decor is predominantly brown: I've never read the upper story. No television. No juke box. No fruit machine.

Kathy looked up from behind the "L" shaped oak bar.

"It's you," said she.
"Indeed it is," said I.
"The usual," said she. A statement, not a question.
"Thank you," said I, as she pulled a stream of porter into the straight sided pint glass.

OK. Kathy's the barmaid. Yes, we haven't seen each other for eighteen years. Or so I think.

"Not been here for a while," said she.
"No," said I.
"How's herself?" said she.

"I haven't seen her for a while," said I.

"Ah," said she.

"How's Tom?" said I.

"Dead," said she. "Nine years now."

"I'm sorry," said I. "He was a good soul."

"Aye," said she. "He's not with you then?"

I thought rapidly. The Professor.

"No," said I. "He's joining me on Monday."

"Will she be coming with him?" said she.

"I think she'll be at home with the weans," said I.

"No," said she, "the young one."

"I don't think so," said I. "Do they come here a lot then?"

"Most weekends," said she. "It's not right, his poor suffering wife cast off like an old toothbrush. And those bairns to consider. I said as much to the new minister."

"New minister?" said I.

"Aye," said she.

"How long's he been here?" said I.

"It's a woman," said she, looking at me pointedly over her glasses. "Ten years come Lammastide. She buried my Tom her first winter here."

"What's she like?" said I.

"She'll be in presently," said she.

"What happened to the old minister?" said I.

"Mr Stuart?" said she. "He's dead and all. Buried in the church yard. Here's your pint."

I took it and sat down at "my" table in the corner.

The old minister was called Stuart? I suppose I knew that. He called once at the cottage but the Professor sent him away with a flea in his cassock.

Over the huge stone fireplace hangs a poor copy in oils of Noel-Paton's celebrated *Bluestane*: the National Gallery in Edinburgh houses the original. I stared at it idly. Along the bottom of the vast frame, cheery peasants overseen by jolly friars haul stones for the partly completed Kirk of Crail, whose spire dominates the centre ground. In the top right hand corner, astride an enormous thunder cloud, the spiteful devil hurls a blue stone plucked from the Isle of May out in the Forth, seen in the background to the left. According to the old tale, the stone split in two in mid-flight. Indeed, one half is still to be found on the shore line behind Tullybothy manse and the other lies to the left of the Kirk gate.

The door opened and a woman of my age strode in. Green waxed jacket. Tweed trousers. Sturdy shoes. Brown hair tied back. She unzipped her jacket revealing the dog collar.

Kathy silently handed her what looked like a large tumbler of whisky.

"Of course they were all Catholics," said she, approaching my table.
"Who were?" said I.
"The people who built the Kirk," said she, pointing at the picture. "People know nothing of Scotland's history. Have you seen *Braveheart*? When I went, the audience seemed to draw its collective breath when it turned out that Wallace wasn't a Protestant. May I join you?"
"Please do," said I.
"So what brings you here?" said she, sitting down opposite me.
"I've borrowed some friends' cottage for a wee break," said I.
"Whose?" said she.

How does one refer to couples? Woman first? Man first? Person one met first, first? Person with most syllables first? Family name as collective noun? And if they're not married?

"Julia and Eric's," said I.

"We're neighbours then," said she. "I'm Frances." and extended a hand.

I shook it and told her my name.

"Have you been to Tullybothy before?" said Frances.

"I used to live here with Eric when we were both undergraduates," said I. "Where are you from?"

"The west," said Frances. "I grew up and went to school in Dunoon and studied at Glasgow. You can see I'm a woman of the cloth. What do you do yourself? You're not from round here."

RBT.

"...so I've been selling books ever since." said I.

"I thought you looked familiar," said Frances. "I really like your shop. I try and go there whenever I'm in the south. So what are you up to here?"

"I needed to finish up some research," said I. "This seemed like a quiet place to get down to it."

"What are you working on?" said Frances.

So many questions! Maybe that's what they teach them in the seminary or whatever they call the Protestant equivalent. Straight to the point. Know your congregation.

What am I working on? Dem bones, dem bones.

"Napier's bones," said I, softly.

"Well there's a coincidence!" said Frances. "You're the second person who's mentioned them to me in the last couple of days."

"Who was the first?" said I.

"Nasty looking customer," said Frances. "He'd obviously heard the local legend. I told him nothing."

"What local legend?" said I.

"Don't you know?" said Frances. "Coincidence on coincidence! He's supposed to be buried here."

But there are no coincidences?

"Who's supposed to be buried here?" said I.

"John Napier," said Frances. "You really didn't know?"

"I'd no idea!" said I. "Wouldn't he have been buried in Edinburgh?"

"You say you're researching him?" said Frances. "You're not very thorough. Apparently his bones were either interred in St Giles or St Cuthbert's, but there no sign of them in St Giles and the original St Cuthbert's is long gone."

"But why would anyone bring his bones here?" said I.

"Napier had a reputation as a wizard," said Frances, "and a lot of his secrets were buried with him. It's said that he built some fiendish weapon."

"That could clear an area four miles round," said I. "Yes, I know."

"Anyway," said Frances, "the story goes that Cromwell wanted to get his hands on it when his army invaded Scotland, so someone on the Covenanting side spirited the coffin away and stashed it here."

"And is the coffin here?" said I.

She paused.

"There's no record of it," said Frances.

"Is that what you told your last visitor?" said I.

She met my eyes and laughed.

"What's your interest?" said Frances.

"I honestly don't know," said I. "I don't know where to begin."

"I don't do confession," said Frances.

"Do you know anything about the epiphany machine?" said I.

"You as well!" said Frances. "That's what the other guy kept going on about. It's a contradiction in terms. Epiphany's a sacred not a mechanical event."

"Have you ever experienced an epiphany?" said I. "Some revelation of Christ's godliness as part of your calling?"

"I once thought I had," said Frances, "but sometimes I suspect it was wind."

"What did it feel like?" said I.

"It was profound and obvious at the same time," said Frances. "It was a recognition of something that I'd probably always known anyway. It felt very good. But I was very young and impressionable. What's all this got to do with machines?"

"An epiphany machine's supposed to engender epiphanies," said I.

"How can a machine invoke divine revelation?" said Frances.

"A machine could cause wind," said I. "If you weren't expecting it you might mistake it for an epiphany. The devil's work, no doubt."

She laughed.

"How old fashioned," said Frances. "False consciousness, surely."

"It depends how broad your concept of an epiphany is," said I. "What about the revelation of Krishna's godhead. Or that that there is no god."

"Back into the mire of relativism," said Frances.

"What about Leary's priests who saw beatific visions on acid?" said I. "There's the real triggering the divine for you."

She laughed again.

"This takes me back!" said Frances. "It's ages since anyone's engaged me in theological disputation. So where does John Napier come into all this?"

"I've no idea what the connection is," said I. "And you never answered my question."

"Didn't I?" said Frances. "I'm a bit pushed for time right now. I've a sermon to write. Why don't you drop by tomorrow after the evening service? Do come to it if you like."

"Thank you but no," said I.

"Opium of the people?" said Frances. "You have no faith to lose and you know it."

"Positively 4th Street?" said I.

"Indeed!" said Frances. "You know he ended up a Christian?"

"That's when I stopped listening to him," said I.

"Is there no virtue in religion at all?" said Frances. "Even Lenin was struck by how reactionary dogma could evoke beautiful works."

"Look," said I, on a whim, "why don't you come for tea tomorrow?"

"Thank you," said Frances. "That'd be nice. What time?"

"When's the evening service over?" said I.

"Around 7," said Frances.

"Around 7 it is," said I.

"Is there anything you don't eat?"

"Any animal protein that isn't the result of transubstantiation," said Frances. "See you the morn then."

She got up, returned her empty glass to the bar and left.

There are no coincidences. So this is how the customer spent the weekend waiting for me to get back from Geneva. I hope he's gone. And I wonder what's in those journal pages the Professor tore out.

I drained the dregs and got up to leave. Too late. The door swung open and Brenda strode into the bar. Her eyes lit up when she saw me.

"My god!" said Brenda. "Where did you spring from? We were talking about you just the other day, weren't we Kathy! How long's it been now? Must be a good seventeen years. Or is it eighteen? It was just before we had the central heating put in."

Kathy silently poured her a large dry sherry.

"How's yourself?" said I. "You're looking well."
"I'm just fine," said Brenda, "but you've certainly aged. You look a lot fatter. And you're really thin on top. Anyway, I'm glad you've shaved that ridiculous beard off. Made you look like a pirate, so Derek always used to say."
"How is Derek?" said I.
"He's dead, poor sausage," said Brenda.
"That's far too young," said I. "I'm sorry."
"So am I when I stop and think about it," said Brenda, "but life goes on. What are you doing now? After you blew your degree you went off to teacher training college, didn't you? Still improving young minds? Or is that too disciplined for you? You never were much good at getting down to anything, were you? One of your endearing features. Just like Peter Pan, so Derek always used to say."

Resistance is useless.

"So what are you up to?" said I. "Still running the bed and breakfast?"
"Gave that up years ago!" said Brenda. "I'm a heritage consultant now. Money for old rope. Literally. All the villages round here are desperate for a tourist attraction and there's loads of lottery money going begging. You go round local farms and cart away all their old implements. Then you clean them up and stick them in the church hall and label them. If you're lucky, you can dredge up some prints of the area and third rate portraits of minor dignitaries. Get the local primary school involved, get the kids to interview their grannies and dig out old family photos. If you're really pushed you can always make a wall display of stuff from the local paper for the last 150 years. Then you commission a retired worthy to research a local history and invent some scenic walks, which you get photocopied. You get someone to make up

a batch of labelled pencils and mugs and tea towels. The local authority sticks up some signs and, voila, you've got a heritage centre!"

"So where's the Tullybothy Heritage Centre?" said I. "I didn't see any signs."

"That bloody woman!" said Brenda theatrically. "Can't she see the place is decaying? But oh no, she won't let me anywhere near her precious church hall. I don't know why I stay here, I really don't."

Across the bar, Kathy raised an eyebrow.

"It's not as if there's much in the way of marketable heritage here," said I.

"You just couldn't be more wrong!" said Brenda, heatedly. "There's heritage everywhere but you have to know how to sell it. Just on the Ness there's Constantine's Cave, and the old tidal mill, and the dock where they tried to put together the original North Carr Light, and the village pump. You've no vision, that's your problem, so Derek always used to say."

"But this place has always been in the shadow of Crail and the old East Neuk villages," said I, "not to mention St Andrews."

"What's St Andrews got to offer apart from a crumbling castle and a third rate aquarium?" said Brenda. "What about all the people who aren't interested in golf? This place has got real potential! I can see it now: the *Fife Ness Experience*. Far more fun than some moth eaten seals and a tank full of herring. But there's no way anyone's going to cough up for a purpose built facility and that stupid bitch won't have any of it."

"Well," said I, "I really must be off."

"Where are you staying?" said Brenda.

"Over the road," said I.

"Oh yes," said Brenda. "In the love nest. I really can't see what she sees in him, you know. He's so aloof, so Derek always used to say. Are you here for long?"

"I'm not quite sure," said I.

"Why now?" said Brenda. "You've never been back before. Has something happened to you? Have you lost your job? Has she finally kicked you out?"

All of the above.

"Just a wee break," said I.
"That'll be right," said Brenda. "Anyway, if you need a cup of tea you always know where to find me."
"Indeed I do," said I. "Thanks."

I smiled wanly at Kathy and left the Inn.

Still not sleepy. Getting chilly.

I went through the kitchen and out the back door. Away from the street lamp, the stars spread across the sky, Cassiopeia and Pegasus, Andromeda beckoning. I opened the coal shed and put a bundle of kindling and two logs in the rusty bucket.

A small mouse writhed between the teeth of the large black cat that shot round my legs into the kitchen. I followed it, shutting the door behind us. In the sitting room, I balled up the centre spread from an aged *East Fife Herald*, layered kindling and lit the fire.

As the flames crisped the yellowing newsprint, were my eyes drawn to the crucial passage? Did I burn my fingers, plucking pages from the pyre? Did I stare transfixed at the toasted text? Ceci n'est pas une libre.

From the corridor, sounds of struggle. The cat had cornered the mouse under the hall chest.

Nature red in tooth and claw. Should I rescue the mouse? Darwinian hubris or the slave's slave?

I collected another beer from the fridge and my bag from the bedroom. Shutting the sitting room door, putting the logs on the fire, taking off my shoes, ensconced cross legged on the sofa, I ring pulled the can and settled down to read.

The handwriting was archaic, but marking endless homework hones character recognition. The notes were essentially a personal diary of Napier's studies in Geneva, turgid torrents of arcane hair splitting. Latterly though, they began to come alive...

...After the morning's lecture, I returned to the book seller in the upper town to see if my order had been delivered. There I encountered the good Dr Stuart of Tullybothy, who enticed me to a Turkish coffee house with promise of novel and original arguments. My old friend fancies himself an Epicurean, a harmless whim in one so upright in spirit. We quickly fell to discussing the new translation of Lucretius. Many of our Faith shun the old texts as at best Superstitious and at worst Heretical: I find them a refreshing change from the dry Popish cant we dispute all day. Lucretius maintains that all is dust and denies our Soul's eternity, an amusing if erroneous conceit. My friend claimed this as licence for unbridled pleasure, a profound misconception as I hastened to point out. Lucretius is neither Ascetic nor Dionysian but seeks a well tempered middle path. In spite of my rebukes, the good Doctor wantonly persisted in his error, citing curious new evidence for the Soul's corporality.

A peasant from the Vaud fell from a hay loft onto a pitch fork. One tine broke off, embedded in the centre of his forehead. All attempts to remove it failed. When his fever broke, he claimed to feel no further pain but complained of strange waking dreams. He was examined by Doctors from the University. His visions were a lucid depiction of Our Lord's Epiphany, unaccountably accurate from one who could neither read nor write. The Doctors endeavoured to extract the tine, to no avail. Bathing the area in hot oil elicited a remarkable change in the unfortunate man's demeanour. At once, beatific serenity was usurped by Hellish auguries of the Last Days, fully in accord with St John's Revelation. Death ensued shortly thereafter.

My gullible friend presented this unlikely tale as further proof of the Soul's tenuous inhabitation of the body. I reminded him that all is vanity and that we shall all face our own Final Judgement in the fullness of Time.

Back in my chambers, I reflected upon his Apocryphal account. In the lives of the Saints we read of Transcendence through great privations, in deserts and caves, on mountains and pillars. Our Dear Lord Himself was tempted for forty days and forty nights and saw mighty Visions but still resisted the blandishments of the Enemy. If lack of food and water or heat by day and cold by night can bring us nearer to Him then why not some other disruption of our Natural State? Might I fashion some Mechanical Device to induce such Understanding in myself? ...

The rest of the manuscript was a dry litany of long forgotten sophistry. The fire burnt briskly. I put down the pages and stared vacantly into the flames.

The flesh mortified? Did Napier ever construct this cunning contraption? Did it work?

The mouse ran into the room, the cat close behind, clockwork conditionings circling the carpet. As the cat pounced, the mouse leapt behind the record stack. The cat crouched low, claws out, eyes ablaze with deep direction.

I put the guard round the fire, went back to my room and collected the Balkan Sobranie box. Opening the back door, I sat on the step and filled the pipe from the bank bag. A good crop that summer, from the geodesic greenhouse: the Professor had a dreadful time trying to shift it. I lit a match and held the flame over the pipe bowl, drawing long and hard. Brain sharp, languor swept the muscles. I exhaled blue against the light from the kitchen window. Relief shivered down the spine. The pipe's glow faded. I struck another match and stirred the bowl, inhaling deeply. Mellowness embraced the frontals. I exhaled and stretched lazily. Waves lapping soft on the shore. Seals barking from the rocks. A shooting star raked the night sky: my wishes never come true.

I tapped the pipe out onto the door step, returned it and the bank bag to the box, and stood up slowly. Time for bed. I shut and locked the back door and turned off the kitchen light. I peered round the sitting room door: no sign of cat or mouse. I turned off the light, leaving the door ajar.

Back in my room, I turned on the main light, put the box back on top of the wardrobe, turned on the bedside light, turned off the main light, undressed quickly, turned off the bedside light and slid between the crisp cold sheets. For a while I lay on my back, vacantly watching the light show on my retinas. Then I curled foetal onto my left side, head nestled on arm, and drowsed off...

>...I was walking on the beach. A naked body was bobbing in the shallows. The seventh wave swept it face down onto the sand, a crucifix birth mark from nape to coccyx and across the shoulders. I turned the body over. The customer leered up at me and handed me a photograph of myself watching myself talking to Felix. "I just sold Cervantes the third volume of 'Don Quixote'," said Felix. "But Cervantes wrote 'Don Quixote'," said I. "Cide Hamete Benengeli wrote 'Don Quixote'," said Felix, "and he stole it from Pierre Menard. Just ask her." Brenda laughed in my face. "You're wasting your time," she said, "but no one can tell you anything, can they." Frances pointed to the bell tower. "Seek and ye shall find," she said, handing me a worn brass key. I opened the tower door, ducked under

the intricate tree of life and mounted the spiral staircase. Each step was steeper than the last and the stairwell steadily narrowed and darkened. There were footsteps approaching fast behind me but my body moved in slow motion from slat to slat. Just as I thought I could climb no further I came out onto a rickety landing with the peal of bells directly above. In the centre of the floor stood an ornate marble catafalque. On top reclined John Napier's effigy. He held a book in one hand, six characters carved into the cover. "A little further to the west," he said, smiling quizzically before shutting his eyes. On the far side of the landing, a man in hose and doublet leant across the balustrade, looking over the village. "Napier's bones," said I softly. The man turned, his hideous horns looming out of the mist, and hurled the huge rock at me...

...I woke in a cold sweat, thick headed, the cat on my chest, daylight seeping through the curtains.

9. On the strand

I shrugged the cat off and got up. The cat meowed and brushed against my legs. I looked at my watch. Nearly 8 a.m. Time for breakfast. I dressed and went through to the kitchen, the cat, tail up, trotting along ahead.

"Nothing here for you, my furry friend," said I, opening the back door.

The cat stood on its hind legs and pawed at the cupboard under the sink. Incredulous, I opened the door revealing a large drum of cat biscuits. I found two saucers, put a handful of green and orange fish shapes into one and water into the other. The cat crunched contentedly. I turned on the front ring, filled the kettle, placed it on the cooker, put a pinch of Assam from the caddy into the tea pot and took a mug from the Welsh dresser.

I'd fair go a couple of four minute eggs. And some toast: brown wholemeal bread with unsalted butter, cut into sodjers.

From the corridor, the mouse scuttled across the kitchen floor, saw the cat and froze. The cat ate steadily. Quickly, I covered the mouse with the mug and slid a glossy brochure for Craigtoun Park twixt rim and lino. Folding the brochure round the mug, I picked them all up and placed them on the back step. Shutting the door behind me, I lifted the mug. The mouse twitched round and darted off into the tall grass.

The kettle began to whistle. I shut the back door, turned off the ring and filled the tea pot. Rinsing out the mug, I sat down at the table and started to pour.

There was a knock at the window. I looked up. Frances beamed back at me. I stood up and opened the door.

"I don't suppose you've seen Hawkins?" said Frances.
"The cat?" said I. "She's just having her breakfast."
"Indeed!" said Frances.
"Would you like something yourself?" said I.
"Thanks," said Frances, "but I never eat before preaching. Anyway, there's nothing to beat freshly blessed host on a Sunday morning."

She bent down and picked up the cat which was studiously washing itself with pre-programmed precision.

"Say thank you to the nice man," said Frances.
"Thank you," said the cat.

I double took.

"Your cat talks!" said I, weakly.
"Of course I talk!" said the cat.
"See you this evening," said Frances, shutting the door behind her.

Fucking weird or what? Frances of Assisi? There are no miracles! Ventriloquism? Wittgenstein says that if lions could talk then we wouldn't understand them.

I sat down and finished pouring the tea.

The world is divided into those who can drink hot liquids straight off and those who can't. I belong to the latter camp. Is it the thickness of the mouth lining? Or the number of heat receptive nerve endings? Or practice, like eating chillies? I hate that blistering of the hard palate which stings like buggery when the burn bursts and peels away leaving raw fresh skin. Not that I've experienced buggery. Is 'stings like buggery' a sign of incipient homophobia? It always involves men but not always with men?

I sipped cautiously at the tea. Just about right. Oatcakes for breakfast? I think not. Maybe I'll walk into Crail. There must be something open. It's strange how Tullybothy's big enough to sustain a church and a pub but not a shop.

I finished the tea, washed up the mug and the saucers, fetched my coat and let myself out of the front door. The street was deserted as I walked south and turned right onto the Crail road at the cross-roads for Danes Dyke and Craighead Farm. On past the site of Balcomie Castle and HMS Jackdaw; once a Fleet Air Arm base; now a cluster of mouldering Nissen huts self-mockingly advertised as a Trading Centre.

At the ramshackle caravan in the lay-by, I stopped and looked back at the vast "W" of sea cleft by the Ness: to the left, the north Tay shore; to the right the Isle of May and the East Lothian coast. In spite of the spoils of war, this is such a pretty place: why did I ever leave? Dorian Graysville.

On we go, south-west down the long straight road to the Balcomie Hotel on the edge of the village: closed for the season. Up Marketgate, past the parish church and the Tollbooth, and onto the High Street where it meets the St Andrews Road.

The *Elite Cafe* was open: I sat down at the table in the window. The menu listed the usual permutations of eggs and bacon and sausages and beans, weakly disguised as an "all day breakfast". It's odd how Americans have more words for cooked eggs than Inuit have for snow.

The waiter approached and hovered expectantly.

"Two four minute soft boiled eggs, brown toast and a large pot of very weak tea with some slices of lemon, please," said I.

He wrote furiously on his pad, echoing each item, and disappeared behind the counter into the kitchen.

Through the window I watched the good burghers of Crail, decked in Sunday finery, off for their tryst with the trinity. Why do they bother? All of the following: catharsis; comfort; duty; fear; guilt; habit; hubris; loneliness; pride; self-righteousness. Did I forget faith and social solidarity?

The waiter returned with a laden tray which he decanted onto the table. Quickly, I put two slices of lemon in the tea cup and topped it up from the pot. Next I spread a slice of toast from the butter pat and cut it into five pieces. Tapping all round the big end of the first egg with the tea spoon, finger tips smarting from the heat, I peeled off the shell which I stowed in the egg cup. The white was firm. Holding my breath, I cut cautiously into the naked top of the egg. Soft yolk! I lightly shook salt and pepper across the wound and plunged in the first strip of bread: salty, toasty, buttery, egginess suffused my mouth. When I'd finished the yolk, I scooped out and ate the white, and pushed the second egg into the empty shell.

"Always eating, aren't you," said Brenda, sitting down opposite me.
"I didn't hear you come in," said I, looking up. "You're not at church then?"
"Don't be bloody silly," said Brenda. "I'm trying to organise a public meeting. Drum up support for my *Fife Ness Experience*."
"Are you getting a good response?" said I.

"The Crail worthies don't want anything to do with it," said Brenda. "They think it's a threat to the local museum. I've been trying to tell them that the Ness is bigger than just Crail but they can't see further than their own pockets."

"So where's your meeting?" said I.

"Tullybothy Church Hall," said Brenda, without irony. "I was just going round sticking up posters when I saw you through the window."

The waiter lurked longingly.

"White coffee, please" said Brenda.

"And some hot water, please," said I.

The waiter repeated our requests and retired.

"What's all this about a local legend linking John Napier to the Ness?" said I, spreading the second piece of toast.

"Completely implausible," said Brenda. "The church is early nineteenth century and Cromwell was up this way over one hundred and fifty years earlier."

"But where did it originate?" said I, slicing off soldiers. "'Local legend' makes it sound like it's steeped in folklore."

"I think it surfaced in one of those crackpot books about secret societies," said Brenda. "You know the sort of thing. The kings of Scotland are direct descendants of Christ through a liaison with a Celtic slave in Roman occupied Galilee, and Free Masonry started in Scotland as a cover for the awful secret, and it's all proved by the hills in the background of *The Monarch of the Glen* which are the same shape as a little known range in Samaria where the remains of an early Christian settlement have recently been excavated."

I smiled appreciatively.

The waiter delivered the coffee and hot water.

Brenda stirred in a spoonful of brown sugar while I revived the tea bag.

"It is a good story, though," said I, trepanning the second egg. "You could use it as part of a heritage theme based on the devil, to link together the Bluestane and Napier the alleged occultist and the smuggling, with *The deil's awa wi the exciseman* playing on the pipes behind a tableaux vivant."
"You're not taking me seriously," said Brenda. "You never did. So superior, so Derek always used to say."

I dusted the darkening yolk. Brenda watched me, pensively supping coffee.

"You know," said Brenda, as I reached for a soldier. "I once thought we had something, you and I."

Mid grasp, I stopped and met her eyes.

OK, after a mid-summer party, under the full moon, amidst the rocks on a patch of silver sand revealed by the receding tide. It felt wonderful. She felt wonderful. I felt wonderful. We felt wonderful. All tenses. No tensions. We made more noise than the seals.

"Did you?" said I.
"How could you do that?" said Brenda.
"Do what?" said I, evasively.

"You know," said Brenda. "Suddenly telling me it was over and just buggering off like that."
"It wasn't sudden," said I. "That was how it was. You knew that."

"You could have been a bit less blunt," said Brenda. "We could have given it another go."

"What would have been the point?" said I. "We weren't going anywhere."

"We could have had a really good relationship," said Brenda, "but you weren't prepared to put anything into it."

"Look," said I. "A relationship isn't something you put things into, like a shopping basket. It isn't even something that you work at, like an exercise bike. It isn't any sort of thing, just a forlorn abstraction. Come to think of it, maybe it is the White Queen's exercise bike; you huff and puff but you never get anywhere, and things happen anyway when you least expect them."

"It was the Red Queen," said Brenda. "Is that all you can do, just hide behind books?"

"But you and Derek were far happier together than we could ever have been, weren't you?" said I. "Why are you doing this now?"

"It was a real shock seeing you again after so long," said Brenda. "It brought it all back. I'd forgotten how much I hated you. And her. For ages and ages. Poor old Derek helped me pick up the pieces. But I suppose it never really went away."

"I'd no idea he was dead," said I. "What happened to him? Had he been ill?"

"He was fixing a hole in the roof," said Brenda. "The wind changed and a gust caught him. He fell off the ladder and landed head first on the railings. Like in that Hitchcock film, *Spellbound*. He hit one of the spikes right between his eyes. It killed him instantly. The strange thing was the look on his face. Not a rictus grin but a huge blissful smile. Just like in *A Voyage to Arcturus*. It was one of his favourite books. You always said it was idealist nonsense. So bloody superior."

There are no coincidences. I said nothing.

"That's a ridiculous way to eat a boiled egg," said Brenda, draining her cup and standing up. "You'd better finish it before it coagulates. I'll see you around no doubt."

She stopped at the door, stuck a notice on the glass panel and strode off without looking back.

The past bisects the present, obviating time travel. But there are too many coincidences and closets full of bones. Soothed by ritual mastication, I paid for my breakfast and Brenda's coffee.

Fresh fruit and vegetables were arrayed in crates on the pavement next door. I put a red pepper, an onion, a lemon and a punnet of mushrooms into a wire basket. In the shop I added a half litre carton of milk, an unsliced wholemeal loaf, a tub of soya margarine and a jar of crunchy peanut butter. Paying the assistant, I put the food into my bag, swung it onto my back and left the shop.

Back along Marketgate, down Kirk Wynd, past the doocot and along the sea front. Through the caravan park: sad rows of green trailer homes, low brick walls disguising wheels, seeking an aura of permanence in jocular name plates. Fly blown wasteland below the airfield, blackberries glistening from brambles between the dune path and the sandstone skerries. Past the gaunt sea stack, I turned into the wildlife reserve: a flock of terns rose from the grassland, wheeling overhead and out to see.

The noise from the breakers slowly grew louder as I neared the Ness. This bay once sheltered a curious commune of breeze blocks and corrugated iron, liberated from the naval station. Ecologically ambiguous, the houses were heated and lit with high octane aeroplane fuel recycled from the subterranean storage tanks. Ostensibly egalitarian, the women soon got fed up with hauling fresh water from the caravan park while the men talked about piping it down the hill. Now, all that's left is Daft Wully's shack, propped hard against the hillside.

Not so daft. Wully had been a teenage peace keeper in one of the endless mittel-European religious wars that scar our century. The first to enter the torture chambers beneath the Klow Palace of Justice, he shot five Syldavian security guards out of hand before his comrades over-powered him. The affair was hushed up and he was airlifted home in a straight-jacket. A year later, he was discharged from Stratheden, Bordurian Order of Kurvi Tasch on his chest, desperate delusion etched into his eyes.

He spent his days combing the coast and snoozing in sandy hollows when it wasn't too wet. At night he tended a fire of driftwood and plastics, unravelling tattered fishing nets into balls of orange twine which he piled at the centre of his hovel, a ruinous repository of compulsive disorder.

Every month he would carry his racing bike up to the main road and pedal into Crail to collect his Dysfunction Allowance from the Credit Dispenser outside the Post Office, re-nationalised only last week by an enlightened Scottish Parliament. Every month the children of Crail chased him out of the village: "Wully! Wully! Where's yer bucket?".

Retreating with engaging dignity, a large sack of oatmeal on the back carrier, he would spend the rest of the day in the *Bluestane Inn*, buying rounds and regaling the regulars with repetitive tales of psychic torment. Once or twice, at closing time, I'd helped him down to the cove with the sack and a crate of bottles of sweet stout, to start the next cycle of sequestered solitude.

As I approached the hut, a small black and white dog rushed at me from behind the wood pile, baring its teeth and barking. I've never liked dogs, well, not since an Alsatian bit my three year old nose in Chiswick High Street. I steeled myself to propel it through the nearest large door but a stern voice shouted "Sit!" and the cur cringed, hunkered on haunches, growling grievously.

"Hello!" said Wully, emerging from the other side of his home.
"Hello," said I. "How's it going?"
"You've come about the bones!" said Wully.
"The bones?" said I. "What bones?"
"They're moving!" said Wully. "Can't you feel them? Come on!".

He dashed into the house. I followed him into the gloom.

"Take these!" said Wully, handing me two candles.

I did so. He struck a match, lit the candles, took one from me, pulled back a feed sack curtain and swung open an iron door in what would conventionally be termed the back wall.

No golden light. A tunnel, lined with white glazed tiles. Cold but dry, air fresh. Narrow gauge railway track.

"This way!" said Wully, shutting the door behind us.
"Where are we going?" said I, as we set off along the wooden sleepers.
"She knows!" said Wully.
"Who knows?" said I.
"She knows!" said Wully. "She looked right into me and she knew straight away!"

The tunnel forked. The tiles and track curved away to the left. Wully took the right hand junction into a darker passage hewn from the sandstone.

"Where are we going?" said I.
"The bones!" said Wully. "You're not like the other one."
"The other one?" said I.
"He asked about the bones," said Wully, "I tried to tell him but he wouldn't listen!"

"Tell me about the bones," said I, patiently.
"They're moving!" said Wully, speeding up. "Can't you feel them? Come on!"

Wully was running now. I wheezed along behind him. Again the tunnel forked. Again Wully took the right hand junction. The floor sloped gently upwards. At the end of the passage, a flight of steps. At the top, Wully dropped his candle and hammered on the studded wooden door with his fists.

"They're moving!" he screamed. "I can feel them! They're moving!"

I bent down to pick up his candle. The fingers of a black woollen glove was sticking out from under the door. I pulled the glove free and inspected it in the flickering flame. No distinguishing marks. No label. I put it in my pocket and relit the candle.

"Come on," said I, gently. "There's no one there."
"But she knows!" moaned Wully. "She looked right into me and she knew!"

I put an arm round Wully's shoulders and slowly guided him back down the tunnel. By the time we reached the entrance, he had re-established some semblance of composure.

"I'm sorry," said Wully, closing the door. "I'm usually all right so long as they leave me alone. But when they start asking about bones it all comes back. I can see them again. Those people. Or what remained of them. I thought they were all dead but I could feel them moving. Then something inside me snapped. But it's all right now."
"Who else knows about the tunnel?" said I.
"Nobody," said Wully, blowing out the candles. "Well, she must know."
"Who must know?" said I, following him outside.
"The new minister," said Wully. "She knows everything. The first time we

met she took both my hands and looked right inside me. Then she smiled and said that she wouldn't tell anyone."

Gnomic gibberish. Is there any point to this rigmarole? Intentional stance.

"Tell anyone what?" said I.
"That there's nothing wrong with me," said Wully. "If anyone found out they'd take away my pension."
"Right," said I. "I'm quite sure she won't tell anyone."
"That's good," said Wully. "You won't either will you."
"No," said I. "Of course I won't."
"Goodbye," said Wully, turning and walking off down to the rocky shore.
"Goodbye," said I to his receding back.

I carried on east towards the Ness. Down the slope between the brambles and onto the point, pausing briefly beneath the Foreland Head light, in front of the concrete pillbox, back to the gun port, facing the North Sea. No more nostalgia. Enough ennui. Round the cliff corner onto the path leading up through Craighead Farm and back into Tullybothy.

The street was still empty. I let myself back into the Professor's cottage. In the kitchen, I put the bag on the table and the kettle on the stove.

I cleaned out the grate, laid and lit a fire, made a large pot of tea and a round of peanut butter sandwiches, and settled down for a lazy afternoon on the sofa with the *Green Child*.

Olivero and Siloën had just descended through the pool's bed of silvery sand into the vast green grotto when I dozed off. Dreamless sleep. Broken by the cat scratching at the seawards window. I checked my watch. Well after six. I stood up, stretched and went through to the kitchen.

"So it's you again," said I, opening the back door.

The cat stared pointedly at the cupboard under the sink.

"I know, I know," said I, filling the saucers.

Without responding, the cat buried its face in the biscuits. Well really, what did I expect, Socratic dialogue?

I took the chopping board and sharp knife out of the drawer, and topped, tailed, skinned and diced the onion. Next I beheaded the red pepper, discarded the stalk and the seeds, and cut the shell into thin strips. Now for the garlic. One clove or two? Two I think: top, tail, skin and slice. I lit the ring under the frying pan and coated it with olive oil which I seasoned with salt, black pepper, dried chilli and the garlic. In with the red pepper and onion: slow sizzled softness. I opened a tin of pinto beans and a tin of chopped tomatoes, and stirred them in with the wooden spatula. Finally, I rinsed the soil from the mushrooms, sliced them into layers across the top of the bubbling broth, put the lid on the pan and turned down the heat.

So far so good.

I swept the detritus into the pedal bin and washed down the board. Then I filled a large pan with cold water, placed it on the second ring and added a drop of the oil. Waiting for Godot, I inspected the sauce. Not so bad; thickening nicely. I stirred in the mushrooms and opened a packet of butterflies. Shells, tubes, wheels, butterflies: I can never remember all the Italian names. Just what is the difference between tagliatelli and fetuccini? As the water came to the boil, I poured in two mugs of pasta and set it to simmer. Lay the table: willow pattern plates - two; forks - two; chocolate spread tumblers - two.

The door bell rang. I went through to the hall and opened the door. Frances smiled from the front step and handed me a large bunch of poppies and cornflowers.

"Thank you," said I. "Do come in."
"Indeed I shall," said Frances. "Something smells good!"

She hung her jacket on the back of the door and followed me into the kitchen.

"Better watch out," said the cat, looking up from the chair. "She's taken her collar off. I bet she fancies her chances."
"Who asked you, you mangy wee shite," said Frances, jocularly.

Just ignore them. Her?

"Do sit down," said I, turning off the rings. "What would you like to drink? There's white wine or beer. Or juice."
"What are we having?" said Frances.
"Pasta with a spicy bean and tomato sauce," said I.
"Red wine would be best," said Frances. "Is that a carafe?", reaching up to the top shelf of the dresser. "I'll just rinse it out."

She removed the stopper and filled the carafe from the cold tap.

"Just the job," said Frances. She poured red liquid into the tumblers and handed me one.

I smelled it cautiously. A heady bouquet. Blackcurrent and cinnamon. Too weird for words.

"Aren't you going to ask me?" said Frances, sitting down.
"Sleight of hand," said I.

"Oh ye of little faith!" said Frances.
"Give the poor bloke a break!" said the cat. "Can't you see he's confused."
"Button your whiskers!" said Frances. "Go on, try it."
"Occam's razor," said I, sipping from the glass.
"Even he believed in miracles," said Frances. "How does it taste?"
"Very good," said I. "But isn't this rather vainglorious for a minister? Party tricks to convert the heathen?"
"There's nothing up my sleeves," said Frances, rolling them back theatrically. "Can we eat now, please? I'm starving."

I forked pasta onto the plates and ladled the sauce over the steaming white mounds.

"Should I say grace?" said I.
"I've had enough prayer for one day," said Frances.

We ate in silence, methodically demolishing my handiwork.

"That was grand!" said Frances finally, pushing back her empty plate. "Any chance of seconds, please?"
"There's no more pasta," said I, "but there's a wee drop of the sauce. And some bread."

I reached over, and took the chopping board and sharp knife from the draining board.

"Let me do that," said Frances.

I handed her the loaf from the bag. She cut off a thick slice, broke it in two and put a chunk on each plate. I covered them with sauce scraped from the bottom and sides of the pan.

"You cook well," said Frances, mouth full. "Are you single?"

"I am now," said I. "What's that got to do with my cooking?"

"In my experience," said Frances, "most single men don't have much idea about how to cook for more than one person."

"What about yourself?" said I.

"Widowed," said Frances. "Just after we got here. A freak wave swept him off the Ness. He couldn't swim, not that he'd have lasted long in that current. The morning tide washed him back to the beach. There were deep red welts across his back where he bounced against the rocks, like a shadow of crucifixion. At the time I drew strength from it. Now I'm not so sure."

Village of women? Far too many coincidences. I looked at her pensively.

"It's OK," said Frances. "One of the few consolations of the cloth is the glimmer that it might not all be totally meaningless. Just a glimmer, mind. More wine?"

She filled both tumblers.

"All right," said I. "I can't stand it any longer. Just where did you learn to do that? I thought that the Magic Circle was one of the last bastions of misogyny."

"Divinity college," said Frances. "And it's not magic."

"Oh come on!" said I. "Water to wine? Surely that's blasphemous."

"You have very strange ideas about Christianity," said Frances. "If Christ could turn water to wine then why not anyone?"

"Are you saying that all ministers can do this?" said I, incredulous.

"Of course they can!" said Frances. "There wouldn't be much point in the Eucharist otherwise, would there."

"Could you teach me?" said I.

"Yes," said Frances, "but I'm not going to."

"Did they show you how to throw your voice as well?" said I.

"Where's the toilet?" said Frances, standing up.
"First on the right," said I.
"Just talk amongst yourselves," said Frances pointedly, shutting the door behind her.

"I think she's offended," said the cat. "You've really stuffed it up."
"Are you talking?" said I. "Or am I hearing you?"
"Both, surely," said the cat.
"But cats don't have enough vocal apparatus," said I.
"Who led the Long March?" said the cat.
"Very droll," said I, getting up and clearing the plates onto the draining board.

Frances returned and sat down.

"Well?" said Frances.
"He's still not convinced," said the cat.
"Would you like a cup of tea?" said I.
"That'd be nice," said Frances. "Weak Earl Gray if you've got any."
"I'll have a look," said I,
"I'll wash up," said Frances.
"No no," said I. "Just leave it.".

But Frances was already at the sink, running the hot tap.

"Scuse I," said I, reaching past her and filling up the kettle.
"Why do you have such difficulty believing your own senses?" said Frances.
"Over exposure to illogical substances," said I.
"Do you usually hear cats talking when you're ripped?" said Frances.
"Not as such," said I. "But it engenders a certain caution. Isn't keeping company with a familiar a sign of witchcraft?"

Frances laughed.

"He's certainly over familiar," said Frances, "but he's no more my familiar than I am his. Anyway, didn't you know that all ministers have cats?"
"I don't know too many ministers," said I.
"Didn't you ever play 'The minister's cat' as a child?" said Frances.
"Where I come from they have vicars," said I.
"The minister's cat is an audacious cat," said the cat.
"The minister's cat is an audacious, belligerent cat," said Frances.
"The minister's cat is an audacious, belligerent, cunning cat," said the cat.
"The minister's cat is an audacious, belligerent, cunning, dastardly cat," said Frances.
"The minister's cat is an audacious, belligerent, cunning, dastardly, engaging cat," said the cat.
"I think he's probably got the idea by now," said Frances.
"'My granny went to market'," said I.
"Precisely," said Frances. "Just the job for a long car journey. How's the tea doing?"

I scrabbled in the cupboard, opening and smelling tins: the Earl Gray commemorated Glasgow City of Culture 1990. I put half a teaspoon of tea into the pot and poured in the boiling water.

"If you'll take this lot through next door," said I, selecting two relatively unchipped mugs from the dresser, "I'll get some more wood for the fire."

10. In the crypt

I collected the bucket, filled it up again from the coal shed and lugged it back to the sitting room. Frances had taken off her shoes and was sitting cross legged on the hearth rug, raking the glowing ashes.

"There's life here yet," said Frances.

I added fresh kindling and a couple of logs. I must remember to chop some more before I leave.

"Shall I be mother?" said Frances, pouring the tea.

I sat down opposite her, cradling a hot mug in my hands.

"So what brought you to Tullybothy?" said I. "It's not exactly a hive of evangelism."
"Internal exile," said Frances. "The Kirk found some of my ideas a bit unorthodox but there's a shortage of ministers and nobody else wanted to come here."
"Which ideas?" said I.
"Well," said Frances. "For starters I'm an atheist."

I stared at her.

"You're an atheist?" said I. "How on earth did you get into divinity college?"
"They never actually ask you what you believe in," said Frances. "They kind of assume that applicants are bursting to spread the word. Anyway, I'm a Presbyterian atheist."
"A Presbyterian atheist?" said I.
"Precisely!" said Frances. "The reformed faith has a far better attitude to women than most churches. And they elect their ministers and elders."
"But how can you stand up and preach something you know is totally contradictory?" said I.
"Come on!", said Frances. "You sell books don't you? In a radical bookshop? Books on pacifism and guerrilla warfare? Books on anarchism and state socialism? Books on lesbian separatism and non-sexist child rearing? You even sell books on atheism and liberation theology! So who's totally contradictory? You can't possibly agree with all of the books you sell."
"But there's no comparison!" said I. "You're in a position of influence."
"So your books don't have any impact?" said Frances. "Why do you bother selling them then?"
"It's a living," said I, feebly. "Surely selling books does some good."
"Just so!" said Frances. "And I'm a badly paid social worker. I bring succour to the poor in spirit. The rest of the time I do pretty well as I please, much like you if half of what Brenda says is true."

I blanched.

"Don't worry!" said Frances. "I've little time for her myself. Well, actually I've lots of time for her. She's lonely and bitter, especially with you. But she's always hard work and lately she's become really tiresome. She goes on and on about the church hall. She thinks that some sort of tourist attraction will breathe new life into the village. But there's lots going on here even if the place is a bit run down. I certainly wouldn't object to a new primary school and a medical centre and even a shop or two. But the last thing we need's a third rate heritage centre!"

"She said you weren't over keen," said I.

"She's right there!" said Frances. "There's nowhere to park. There aren't any public toilets. There's no cafe. Can you see Kathy agreeing to serve cream teas in a fishwife's bonnet? There's nothing here that you can't find somewhere else already. Vikings and smugglers and nineteenth century industrial sites are old hat. Constantine's Cave's dank and smelly. Not even Wully goes in there. You must know Wully."

"I bumped into him this morning," said I. "Seemed much as I remembered him. Why's he so wary of you?"

"His mother asked me to see him just after I got here," said Frances. "She'd given up on the shrinks years ago and wanted me to exorcise him. He is an obvious candidate for de-conditioning but he actually quite likes his life. Anyway, what would he do with himself? He's completely unemployable. And he doesn't do anyone any harm as he is."

"So what about the Napier story?" said I. "Is there really nothing to it?"

"It's complete nonsense," said Frances. "The church is far too young. Ask Brenda."

"So there's no sign of anything there?" said I.

"Have you ever actually been in the church?" said Frances.

"I have not," said I.

"Come and have a look!" said Frances.

"Now?" said I.

"No time like the present," said Frances.

She put on her shoes and gathered up the cups and teapot. I put the guard in front of the fire. We met in the hall. I put on my coat and opened the front door.

"Thanks again for the food," said she, stepping out into the yellow light. "Thanks for washing up," said I, shutting the door behind us. "Lead on."

Lots of doors to open and shut in cold climates. Scandinavians often comment on how badly Scottish houses are organised given the prevailing weather: no double glazing; little central heating; less roof insulation. Scotland is really a Mediterranean country: it would never have drifted so far north it hadn't been forced to share a tectonic plate with perfidious Albion. Roll on global warming. When none of us will have air conditioning.

We walked down the street and through the gate into the churchyard. In the porch, Frances turned on the lights, took a large key off a hook by the notice board and let us both into the church.

Bare white plaster walls. Hammerbeam roof. North wall plaque commemorating the Skelly disaster. Ten rows of wooden pews. Harmonium. Plain white altar cloth over a simple stone plinth; polished brass crucifix; wildflowers in a green glaze vase.

"What do you think?" said Frances.
"It's a wee bit austere," said I.
"No distractions," said Frances. "Just the flock and their shepherd. Anyway, there wasn't much money left over when they'd finished it."
"When was it built?" said I.
"Eighteen fourteen," said Frances. "They got Alexander Leslie to design it, you know. He was good. He did Ceres and Kilrenny as well. Do have a look round."
"Is there a crypt?" said I.

Frances paused.

"Not exactly a crypt," said Frances. "More of a cellar. Full of rubbish. Nothing of any interest."

I took the glove out of my pocket.

"Nothing of any interest?" said I, proffering it to her.

"That's funny," said Frances nonchalantly, taking the glove, "I've already got one just like this."

"The old ones are the best," said I.

"Indeed they are," said Frances, heading back to the porch. "Come and give me a hand then."

She rolled back the brown coir mat: two large iron rings set into the wooden floor. Frances crouched and grasped one ring with both hands: I took the other.

"One, two, three, lift!" said Frances.

We raised the hatch and swung it to one side, revealing a broad stone staircase.

"Down we go," said Frances, descending the steps.

"No rush lights?" said I, following her.

"All mod cons," said Frances, turning on the fluorescent strip.

The stair well came out into a rectangular space which seemed much larger than the church above. Frances stepped into the centre of the crypt. I joined her.

"I think this may be what you're after," said Frances.

Flush with the floor, a dull grey slate slab:

> MDL – IOANNE NEPERO - MDCXVII

I read the inscription over and over again; studied the cherub holding an hour glass leaning against the skull.

"Well say something," said Frances, after a while. "'Thank you' would do for starters."
"Thank you," said I, mechanically.
"You're welcome," said Frances. "Is that all?"

Is that all? Napier's bones?

"What's inside?" said I.
"I've no idea," said Frances. "I've never looked."

I squatted down and ran a finger along the top edge of the stone.

"Someone has," said I. "There's a lip just here. Have you got a crowbar?"
"There's one in the porch," said Frances. "Don't go away."

She disappeared upstairs. I looked around. Studded door on the far wall; must be the one that thwarted Wully. Single row of wooden seats with continuous high backs along the left and right hand walls.

Frances quickly rejoined me, carrying a crowbar and a torch.

"Tell me again why we're doing this," said Frances.
"Haven't I told you?" said I, disingenuously.
"No," said Frances, "you haven't."
"Now?" said I.
"Yes now," said Frances firmly, leaning on the crowbar.
"We'd best sit down," said I.

RBT.

"...and I really didn't know there was any connection with Tullybothy at all until you mentioned the legend," said I.

"Assuming for a moment that the utterly improbable account you've just given me has even the slightest basis in reality," said Frances, "what can there possibly be in a seventeenth century tomb that's relevant to your epiphany machine?"

"I haven't the faintest," said I.

"We better have a look then," said Frances.

"Just like that?" said I.

"Just like that!" said Frances, standing up and passing me the crowbar.

"Don't you want to do it?" said I.

"No no," said Frances. "It's your mystery. You go ahead."

I slipped the splayed end under the lip and pushed down steadily on the lever. The slab edge began to lift. I slid the crowbar further in and raised the end of the cover above the level of the floor.

"I don't know what to do now," said I. "I don't want to drop the crowbar into the tomb."

"How heavy's the stone?" said Frances.

"It moved fairly easily," said I.

"Maybe we could shift it sideways," said Frances. "Just enough to look inside. I'll get the grave digger's planks and we can slip them under the corners. I'll not be a minute."

I gently lowered the cover, extracted the crowbar and studied the crypt more closely.

The walls don't look right for a Georgian building; they must be far older than the church, older than the tombstone. Think carefully. We're not actually under the church. The stairs run south. And the door's on the wall opposite the stairs, which must be nearer the cliff face. The seating's reminiscent of a medieval choir stall. I wonder if there are misericords?

I lifted up a seat: livid dorsal vein, foreskin retracted, the bronze phallus swung up at a jaunty forty-five degree angle, life size if mine is anything to go by. I lifted up the next seat: delicate labial folds surmounted the swelling bronze pudendum.

"They're all like that," said Frances, coming down the stairs. "Let's get on with it then. Don't just stand there gawping."

I hurriedly folded down the seats and took up the crowbar. As I levered up the end of the slab, Frances wedged a plank under each corner. I released the crowbar, walked round to the other end, felt along the edge and found another lip. In with the crowbar. Up it goes. Two more planks in place.

"Let's try sliding it," said Frances.

One at each end, legs apart, bending down, grasping corners.

"To my right," said Frances. "Steady now."

Slowly we eased the stone sideways. The inside of the tomb was in shadow. I turned on the torch and swept the light along the opening.

A skeleton, arms crossed on chest. Headless.

"Curiouser and curiouser," said Frances, taking the torch and playing it above the topmost vertebra.

Six familiar characters, inscribed in black ink on the wooden board where the head once lay.

"This is all too weird," said I, shaken.

"What's all too weird?" said the customer, coming down the stairs into the crypt.

"I told you to stay away!" said Frances.

"You told me!" said the customer, advancing towards us. "What have you found?"

"There's nothing here!" said I, desperately.

"Aren't you dead yet?" said the customer, peering into the grave. "Give me the torch. Now."

"Look not behind thee!" shouted Frances, throwing the torch over his head.

The customer froze mid turn, twisted round, lunging for the torch.

"King James version," said Frances. "Always works."

"What have you done to him?" said I, retrieving the torch.

"Behold he looked back from behind her, and he became a pillar of salt," said Frances.

"You've turned him to salt?" said I. "But you can't!"

"Why can't I?" said Frances. "I just have, haven't I?"

"But he's alive tomorrow!" said I. "He must be! Or I can't be here!"

Frances looked nonplussed.

"Why do I get the feeling you haven't told me everything?" said Frances.

"Well, you didn't tell me everything, did you?" said I.

"I'll show you mine if you show me yours," said Frances.

"Fair enough," said I. "Shall we roll back the rock?"

RBT.

"...so it's all a bit hard to get the brain round," said I, heaving down on the crowbar. "I suppose it's some sort of temporal displacement though I've no idea what causes it."

"Well," said Frances, removing the last plank. "you are here. So he must be alive in Edinburgh tomorrow. No wonder he's going to be so angry with you! Are you quite sure you're there now as well?"

"I don't know," said I, easing the slab down off the crowbar. "I could always phone and check."

"It would be so much easier just to dump him here," said Frances. "But if you really think we can't, I can always rehydrate him. Could we carry him?"

"We could try and use a couple of planks like a stretcher," said I. "but it'd be really awkward. I don't know if we'd get him up the stairs in one piece."

"Let's stick him in the tunnel," said Frances.

She unbolted the studded door. Carefully, we picked up the customer, carried him through and propped him up against the wall.

Standing by the body, Frances intoned: "For every one shall be salted with fire, and every sacrifice shall be salted with salt. Salt is good: but if the salt have lost his saltiness, wherewith will ye season it? Have salt in yourselves, and have peace with one another."

The customer shuddered a single mighty spasm and collapsed onto the floor.

"He'll be fine," said Frances. "Wully'll let him out."

We went back into the crypt and she bolted the door behind us.

"What on earth was that last stuff?" said I.
"Mark Chapter 9, Verses forty-nine and fifty," said Frances.
"What does it mean?" said I.
"Just what it says," said Frances. "Anyway, we'd best tidy up, not that anyone ever comes down here."

Oh yes.

Frances collected the crowbar and torch while I stacked the planks. Back in the porch, we lowered the hatch and straightened the matting. Frances stowed the burgling kit in the cupboard under the bench.

"I should never have left them on," said Frances, turning off the lights. "Aye well. The wood goes round the side. This way."

I deposited the planks by the church wall.

"Thank you," said I. "You've been great."
"I'm afraid you're not much further on," said Frances. "Have you time for a night cap?"
"That would be nice," said I.

We left the churchyard. By the gate stood a blue VW. I checked the number plate.

"Not so good," said I.
"Is that his car?" said Frances.
"I suppose it must be," said I.
"You don't sound too sure," said Frances.
"I'm not," said I.
"Have you seen it before?" said Frances.
"I have," said I, "but I thought its owner was dead."

Silently, we walked back through the village to the manse. Frances let us in.

"Do come through," she said, opening an oak panelled door off the hall. "A wee dram?"
"Just the job," said I, following her.

"Do sit down," said Frances, gesturing towards a battered brown leather arm chair.

I did so. She took a decanter and two thistle cut glasses from the sideboard, poured two healthy measures, passed me one and sat down in my chair's twin.

"Slainte!" said Frances, raising her glass.
"Slainte mhath!" said I, toasting her.
"Not bad for a Sassenach," said Frances.
"Praise indeed!" said I. "What are we drinking?"
"*The Smith's Glenlivet,*" said Frances. "Nothing but the best for the Lord's anointed."
"You've expensive tastes, you clerics," said I. "It's no wonder old Henry wanted to nationalise you."

We sipped, leisurely regarding each other.

"It's a bit cold down here," said Frances. "How about a bed time story?"
"What are you reading?" said I.
"*The Song of Solomon,*" said Frances.
"I'm not sure that's wise," said I.
"What's wrong?" said Frances. "I won't eat you."
"You don't know where I've been," said I.
"That's all right," said Frances. "I've loads of condoms."
"You don't quite understand," said I.
"Not more of this rigmarole," said Frances. "You make religion sound plausible. Do tell."

RBT.

"...There's no test but I've been symptom free for more than four days so maybe I am clear?" said I.

"Salt?" said Frances thoughtfully. "Do you want to be a pillar of the community?"

"I'm no hamster," said I, "but I suppose it might work. Are there side effects?"

"Only if you don't change back," said Frances. "Do you want to give it a go?"

"Are you sure it's safe?" said I.

"Of course it's safe!" said Frances. "Trust me, I'm a minister."

That's an argument? Am I that eager to exchange body fluids?

"You don't mind?" said I.

"Not at all," said Frances. "Now?"

"Fire away," said I.

"Look not behind thee" said Frances softly.

I turned round, tingling...

    I can't see anything.

    I can't hear anything.

    I can't feel anything.

    I can't smell anything.

    Nothing!

    "Am I dead?" said I.

    "Do you feel dead?" said the voice.

    "I'm not sure," said I. "I've never been dead before."

    "Why do you think you might be dead?" said the voice.

"I think I've just been turned to salt," said I.

"How very fitting," said the voice, "for a *Green Child* enthusiast. Don't they all end up becoming one with the crystalline rocks? Of course it's all much older than Genesis. Coyote could turn people into red sandstone. Then there's always Midas and Medusa..."

"This is all very erudite," said I, "but if I'm dead, just how am I having this conversation?"

"Are you having a conversation?" said the voice.

"Of course I am!" said I. "What else am I doing?"

"Cogito ergo sum?" said the voice. "Didn't get Descartes very far, did it."

"Am I still alive then?" said I.

"Were you ever alive?" said the voice.

"Of course I was!" said I. "I expect to be so again fairly soon."

"How's that?" said the voice. "Transmigration of souls? Resurrection? Reincarnation?"

"I don't know what the exact mechanism is," said I.

"You're very trusting," said the voice, "to be turned into salt on some vague understanding that you'll be turned back again. How do you know it'll work at all?"

"I've seen it done once already," said I.

"Are you sure that's what you saw?" said the voice. "Do you believe everything you see?"

"Look," said I. "Just who are you?"

"Who would you like me to be?" said the voice. "I can be St Peter in a long white robe. I can be a bureaucrat at a desk. I CAN BE DEATH IN CAPITAL LETTERS. I can be Vergil. I can be Charon. I can be the collective unconscious. Choose your tradition."

"Is it a free market then?" said I.

"Isn't everything since 1989?" said the voice.
"So just what is going on?" said I.
"Mark Twain put it quite well," said the voice. "'*Nothing exists save empty space - and you!* And you are not you - you have no body, no blood, no bones, you are but a *thought.*'"

...and slumped back into the chair. It was dark, then dawn. Frances stood over me holding a blanket.

"Are you all right?" said Frances.
"I think so," said I, feeling myself all other. "Have I been here all night?"
"I'm rather afraid you have," said Frances.

Rejected. Despised. A man of sorrow.

"Why did you change your mind?" said I.
"I didn't," said Frances. "Something came up."
"Something came up?" said I. "What came up?"
"You better come and have a look," said Frances.

We went back outside. The blue car's gone. The cottage door's open. Straight to the bedroom. The bag's still there. Check inside.

"He's taken the journal pages," said I, carefully inspecting *The Green Child*.
"Does it matter?" said Frances.
"I'm not sure," said I, putting the book back into the bag. "What exactly happened?"
"I was about to restore you," said Frances, "when I heard an almighty crash. I rushed out here but I couldn't see anything. Hawkins said he was round the back but by the time I'd got there he was out the front door. I covered you up and phoned the police."

"Couldn't you have stopped him?" said I.
"I'm a minister," said Frances. "I can feed the five thousand but I'm not Wonder Woman."
"Why didn't you revive me?" said I.
"Half the village was up," said Frances. "It wouldn't look very good, would it?"
"I suppose not," said I. "But didn't they ask where I was?"
"Why would they think that I knew where you were?" said Frances.

We went through to the kitchen. The back door lay on the floor.

"But it wasn't even locked!" said I.
"Dramatic effect," said Frances, inspecting the door. "Come and have a look. These hinge screws are really tiny. It looks like they ripped straight out. I'm astonished that it's stayed up for so long."

She checked the frame.

"I think we can put in some longer ones if we drill the holes out a bit first."
"There used to be some tools in the shed," said I, going outside.

We spent the best part of an hour putting the door back up. As I swept up the dust from the drilling, Frances made tea.

"I'm all in," said I, sitting down. "I could really do with some sleep."
"It's not exactly relaxing, is it?" said Frances, pouring the tea.
"What isn't?" said I.
"Being turned to salt," said Frances.
"You've tried it?" said I.
"Oh yes," said Frances. "We all had to as part of our training. What did you encounter?"
"There was a voice," said I.

"What sort of a voice was it?" said Frances. "The voice of doom? The voice of authority? A heavenly choir?"

"It was just a voice," said I. "It quoted Mark Twain. *The Mysterious Stranger.*"

"Death's wasted on solipsists," said Frances.

"So I was dead?" said I.

"Well you weren't very alive, were you?" said Frances.

And death shall have no dominion? I sipped at the tea. The bones.

"What time is it?" said I.

"Going on six," said Frances.

"I've got to be in Edinburgh early this evening," said I, thinking aloud frantically. "And there mustn't be any sign that I've been here when I come back with the Professor."

"Is Eric a Professor?" said Frances.

"Of course he isn't!" said I. "Look, I've really blown it, haven't I! Lots of people know I've been here for the last couple of days but he knows I've been in Edinburgh with him."

"Both are true, aren't they?" said Frances. "Anyway, what does it matter?"

"But if he knows it'll affect what happens next," said I.

"Everything you ever do affects what happens next," said Frances, calmly. "You've been in an unnaturally privileged position where you've known in advance quite a lot of what's going to happen. You're trying to get back to what you think is normal and you're frightened of any deviation. But anything you might do has potential repercussions and you don't actually know what's going to happen in fine enough detail to have any confidence in anything you do. Suppose you've forgotten something? What if something unexplained happened last time and it might have been you intervening this time that caused it? Should you intervene now? What if you do and it wasn't you? What if you don't and it was you? It's not very liberating, is it, hanging around waiting for what you know's going to happen to happen. This evening all that stops and you're flying blind again, just like the rest of us."

Ignorance is bliss? But we understand an apple by eating it, and the world by changing it.

"That's little comfort," said I. "I thought you lot dealt in certainties."
"Us lot?" said Frances.
"Presbyterians," said I. "Don't you believe in predestination?"
"Not any more," said Frances, "I think I'm probably an existential humanist. Anyway, who needs labels?"
"That's just what Felix said," said I.
"Who's Felix?" said Frances.

How to explain?

"He's someone I met in Geneva," said I.

Frances looked at me strangely.

"Felix?" said Frances. "In Geneva? Not the bookseller?"
"You know Felix?" said I, aghast. "How do you know him?"
"I think my predecessor must have been writing a history of the area," said Frances. "When I finally got around to clearing out the attic there was a box of old books and I found Felix's card in one of them. When I phoned, he said he'd sold most of them to Stuart in the first place and he'd be happy to buy them all back."

No coincidences, eh?

"So Felix has been here?" said I.
"Of course he has," said Frances. "There was no way I was going to post all those books to Switzerland."

"So when was he here?" said I.

"It must have been four or five years ago," said Frances.

"How big was he?" said I.

"What a peculiar question!" said Frances. "Come to think of it though, he was really very thin."

"Felix Haddock?" said I.

"The same!" said Frances. "What's this all about?"

Damned if I know. No, I'm not going to tell her. Not yet anyway.

"How did he get here?" said I.

"That's the strange thing," said Frances. "He just turned up. There was no sign of a car or a taxi. I suppose he must have walked from Crail. When he'd been through the books he asked to look round the churchyard. I went back to the manse for something and by the time I returned he was gone."

"Is the old minister buried here?" said I.

"In the family mausoleum," said Frances. "There'd always been a Stuart in the manse, father and son, until I came along. He was the last one."

Sounds like a Timeline booth. Might come in handy, not that my sylph like form can stand much more travelling. But didn't Felix say that the Stewart connection was a coincidence?

"What books did he take back?" said I.

"They were all pretty obscure," said Frances. "Mostly local accounts written by eigtheenth and nineteenth century Fife ministers. Oh, there was a rather nice translation of Ovid's *Medea*."

"Ovid's *Medea*?" said I. "That's supposed to have been lost in antiquity."

"I had a quick browse," said Frances, "and it looked quite interesting. It's all written from Medea's point of view. I'd have kept it but he insisted I included it with the others."

"I hope you got a good price for it," said I.

"I don't remember," said Frances. "It all went into the Kirk roof fund."

Fruit flies like a banana: Edinburgh calling.

"I don't suppose you're driving into St Andrews today?" said I.
"I don't have a car," said Frances. "You could ask Brenda."
"I think not," said I. "There's always the thumb."
"Well," said Frances, "I'd best be going. I've souls to salve."
"Thanks again for all your help," said I.
"Think nothing of it," said Frances.
"It'll be good to meet up with you again," said I.
"I've no plans to go anywhere," said Frances. "Fare forward, voyager."

Will the fire and the rose be one? She let herself out.

I packed up the kitchen, unmade my bed, cleaned out the fireplace, put the milk and bread and peanut butter and marge and flowers into the bag, bolted the back door, turned off the electricity and left the cottage.

11. On the bench

Out of the village and onto the high road.

Grey skies, fallow fields. Sunlight bleeding through low haar. Anxious, ill at ease. Sound of a car. Stick out the thumb. It overtakes and stops.

"Where are you off to?" said Brenda, leaning out of the window.
"Edinburgh," said I.
"I can drop you near the St Andrews bus station," said Brenda, opening the door. "In you get."
"Thanks!" said I, getting in.

"So that really was a wee break," said Brenda, accelerating.
"No no," said I, fastening the seat belt. "I'll be back this evening."
"Why not just stay?" said Brenda.
"Things to clear up," said I.
"I won't ask," said Brenda.

Too tired for small talk.

"Why do you stay?" said I.
"I suppose I could have left when poor old Derek died," said Brenda, "but I really rather like it here."
"You never met anyone else?" said I.

"That would be telling," said Brenda archly. "How are things with you two?"
"You were right," said I, "though it's nearly two years since she left."
"Are you still in touch with her?" said Brenda.
"No," said I. "Well yes, but only in the last couple of days."
"Last time I saw her she cut me dead," said Brenda. "Stuck up bitch."
"She does tend to form firm opinions of people," said I.
"Where is she now?" said Brenda.
"French Alps," said I. "Near Geneva."
"All right for some," said Brenda.

Past the Randerston turning. Years ago I spent the winter break here, house sitting. We came down one frosty morning to find Lafayette the parrot strutting up and down his kitchen floor; Korky the budgerigar lay stiff on the bottom of the cage. We'd forgotten to put the heater on overnight.

"It's funny," said Brenda. "It's been years, literally, but it feels like it's only yesterday since we last saw each other."
"It is," said I.
"You know what I mean," said Brenda. "You certainly seem much the same."
"So do you," said I. "I'm just surprised you're still so angry after all this time."
"I loved you," said Brenda.
"Loving someone doesn't give you any claims on them," said I.
"So what else does?" said Brenda.
"Reciprocity," said I.
"You don't believe that," said Brenda.
"If you say so," said I.
"Don't you judge me!" said Brenda.
"You know we can't agree," said I. "Let's drop it."

Through Kingsbarns. Make an effort.

"What are you up today?" said I.

"Seeing a client in Forfar," said Brenda.

"*The Bridie Experience?*" said I.

"You're so bloody clever, aren't you," said Brenda. "Do you have any idea how may bridies get eaten every day? It's a vital part of Scotland's culinary heritage."

"You don't have to sell it to me," said I. "Do you remember those awful curried bridies they used to sell in the Union? Yellow with curry powder, oozing oil."

No response. Round Pitmelly and down to Boarhills.

"You've never asked about Jake," said Brenda.

"Jake?" said I. "The wean! I'm sorry, I'd completely forgotten! Hardly a wean now. What's he like?"

"Come and meet him," said Brenda. "It would be good for him to get to know his father."

This isn't happening.

"What do you mean?" said I. "Derek was his father."

"No," said Brenda. "You are. I realised I was pregnant about three weeks after you dumped me."

"Why didn't you tell me?" said I.

"Would it have made any difference?" said Brenda. "How would I have felt if it had?"

"Did Derek know?" said I.

"Of course he knew!" said Brenda. "Poor dull Derek, with his green gumboots and his mouse mat collection. How you all sneered at him."

Up past Kinkell, approaching the Braes.

Did this really happen or am I *Timeline*d? Same difference. Did this really happen this *Timeline*? Why would she lie? Why tell me now?

"You're sure he's mine?" said I.
"Of course I'm sure!" said Brenda. "What the hell do you want, a DNA test?"
"What do you expect of me?" said I.
"I don't expect anything," said Brenda. "Do what you like. You always have done."

Down past the Brownhills Garage and the Gatty Marine Laboratory.

…The gaunt stranger stepped into the light: "My son! My son! At last I have come home!" The young man looked up: "Father! Oh father, is it really you?"…

Round the city wall. City walls?

"Does Jake know?" said I.
"Not yet," said Brenda. "But it's nearly his eighteenth birthday and I've always said I'd be totally honest with my children."
"Why do you want to tell him?" said I. "Just to get back at me?"
"That's despicable!" said Brenda.

Indeed. Onto South Street.

"Have you discussed this with Frances?" said I.
"I have," said Brenda.
"What did she say?" said I.
"Ask her yourself," said Brenda, "if what she thinks is so much more important to you than what I'm telling you."

Right at the roundabout.

"I'm sorry," said I. "I'm finding this all a bit hard to get my brain round."
"There's lots of time," said Brenda. "All right if I drop you round the corner?"

Left into Market Street.

"Sharing half my genes isn't much of a basis for anything," said I. "He really is Derek's son. You both brought him up, after all. What have I got to offer him?"
"Nurture not nature?" said Brenda, drawing up outside the old Union building. "That's a cheap rationalisation. I'd hoped for better."
"Do what you think is best," said I, unbuckling the belt and opening the door. "I'm easy to find if he wants to find me. I'm still the only one in the Edinburgh phone book. If he gets in touch then I'll give it a go."
"Roch the win'," said Brenda.

I got out. She drove off. I walked to the end of the road and right down the hill to the bus station.

The Edinburgh bus isn't due to leave for nearly an hour. *The Victoria Cafe* used to do a decent breakfast.

Back to the Union and over the road. *Victoria Cafe? Cafe Diana.* Up the stairs and into the dining room. Huddles of language school students nursing hangovers. I approached the bar and scanned the chalk board.

"Cheese and ham croissant, and a large pot of weak Earl Gray with lemon, please," said I.
"Where are you sitting?" said the young woman.
"By the window," said I.
"I'll bring it over," said the young woman.
"Thank you," said I.

I sat down. Someone had left the *The Scotsman* on the gingham tablecloth, the crossword all but completed. I haven't tried it regularly since I stopped commuting to Glasgow all those years ago. I read the remaining clue:

31 across - Boar's pennies? You can count on them! (7,5)

The microwave bell rang. Always a bad sound.

The young woman put the tray onto the table. Gingerly, I poked at the croissant. Steamed face cloth; yellow mastic; pink rubber. I raised the lid and peered into the teapot. Two bags. Stewed. No sign of lemon. I poured a cup and topped it up from the jug: the cream promptly curdled. Sighing, I returned to the counter, and requested a pot of hot water and a clean cup.

When I'd finished my profoundly disappointing repast, I paid the bill and returned to the bus station. The Edinburgh bus sat at the stand, 'Local service' on the destination display. Wait another hour or so for the express? Indecisive, I hovered by the open door.

"Either you're on the bus or off the bus," said the driver.
"On the bus," said I, ascending the step and paying the fare.

The bus was dingy, floor dirty, windows fogged, seat fabric worn and tattered; further proof, were any needed, of the benefits of privatisation. Sit at the back and try to snooze. Eventually, the bus lurched off. No crow's flight; three hours of fitful sleep: Jake, Brenda, Frances, Felix, Guardbridge, the wheels on the bus go round and round, Dairsie, bones, epiphanies, bones, epiphanies, Cupar, dodeska-den, dodeska-den, Ladybank, Jake, Brenda, Frances, Felix, Collessie, we're going to be late, we're going to be late, Auchtermuchty, bones, epiphanies, bones, epiphanies, Gateside, the wheels on the bus go round and round, Kinross, Jake, Brenda, Frances, Felix, Kelty, dodeska-den, dodeska-den, Lochgelly, bones, epiphanies, bones, epiphanies, Cowdenbeath, we're going to be late, we're going to be late, Crossgates, Jake,

Brenda, Frances, Felix, Dunfermline, the wheels on the bus go round and round, Rosyth, bones, epiphanies, bones, epiphanies, Inverkeithing, dodeska-den, dodeska-den, North Queensferry and over the Forth Road Bridge to Edinburgh.

I alighted at Haymarket, trudged up Morrison Street, through Tollcross and onto the Meadows. Early afternoon. I'm on Blackford Hill and so's the Professor so it's safe to go home.

I let myself in and put the food into the fridge. Next, I put my initials on the fly sheet of the *Timeline* manual and carefully shelved it in the travel books between Thailand and Torres Straits. *The Green Child* was already on the shelf. Two copies? But one's about to leave?

The answerphone light was blinking. I pressed 'play':

"Thanks for the letters."

She is alive. So have I sent her the password? Not yet. How? *Timeline*? I'm not very keen to travel anymore. "Thanks for the letters." Ambiguity. Do I send her lots of copies?

I went round the corner to the office supply shop: one ream of sixty gm A4 paper, one hundred plain brown envelopes, seven A4 sheets of sticky labels. From the post office next door: one hundred first class pound stamps, one hundred airmail stickers. Two frantic hours of kitchen-table-top publishing: one hundred copies of the dubious digits; one hundred address labels. A further hour: a neat stack of sealed, addressed, stamped envelopes. Time is pressing: I've no wish to meet myself. Or be incinerated.

Straight up Marchmont Road and into the Grange cemetery. No one around. Back with the fronds, into the lift and down to the phone:

"Thank you for choosing *Timeline*," said the androgynous mid-Atlantic voice. "When instructed, select 1 to reverse time; select 2 to bifurcate time; select 3 to freeze time. Select now, please."

I did nothing.

"You have not made a selection," said the voice. "For other services please insert a credit card."

I swiped the Book Token card into the reader.

"To travel, select 1. To travel backwards, select 2..." said the voice.

I pushed:

   2

"Please enter your destination code," said the voice.

I punched in:

   436382

"Please enter your destination date as two day digits, two month digits and as many year digits as you require, positive or negative, according to the Christian convention," said the voice.

I punched in last Wednesday's date, opened the exit and threw the envelopes, one by one, into the golden light of the quantiverse. Fare forward, voyagers. I shut the exit and returned to the entrance.

The gate creaked open. I must be coming. I dashed down a side path, crouched low behind a granite angel and watched myself escape.

The customer and his companion came into the graveyard.

"The swine's got away again," said the customer.
"You shouldn't talk about him like that," said his companion.
"It's nothing personal," said the customer.

They left together by the north gate. I waited a while, and set off through the south gate towards Lovers Loan.

Did the mail get through? The answerphone says it did. What would have happened if I hadn't sent the letters? While not impossible, it's highly improbable that they would have materialised out of the ether. So I must have sent them eventually. As indeed I have.

Back in the flat, I fired up the mighty Wurlitzer, surfed for the Museum, menued up the 'Search' form and typed in:

epiphany machine

This service is temporarily unavailable. Please try again later.

Mission accomplished or system glitch? No way of telling. Anyway, where was I when I was so rudely interrupted? I'd just collected the keys from Julia. I need to find the Professor.

I checked the book shelf for *The Green Child*. Lost in the loop. I took it out of my bag and carefully put it back.

I shut up the flat and shambled over the Meadows. In the Grassmarket, the gate was open and the light was on in the laboratory. I went in. The Professor and his assistants huddled forlornly round a workstation.

"It's a complete fucking disaster!" said the Professor. "Five years fucking work gone! Surely someone kept a backup?"

Scratchit looked at Itch. Itch looked at Scratchit.

"You said we shouldn't be connected to the Department's network," said Itch.
"They'd have backed us up automatically every evening," said Scratchit.
"But you said we needed to maintain complete secrecy to satisfy the client," said Itch.
"And you said we should never keep any copies of anything," said Scratchit, "in case they fell into the wrong hands."

They shrugged at each other, and returned to their pods.

"What's happened?" said I.
"The entire fucking project's vanished," said the Professor. "Some bastard's hacked us and wiped the fucking thing."

There are no coincidences.

"What was the project?" said I.
"Virtual reality," said the Professor. "For the museum. They've lost loads of visitors since they introduced entry charges so they're trying to present their collections through 3D models in a totally immersive environment. I don't really know much about the details. I just hold the grant. Those two do all the work."
"Who's paying for it?" said I.
"Sinclair-Laker," said the Professor. "They're matching money from the Lottery but they're retaining commercial rights to the software. They think

there's a really big potential for home entertainment. Oh, they insisted that I employ those two."

A likely story. No, not irony.

"So why didn't you wait for me?" said I.
"I couldn't face her," said the Professor. "Surely you can see that?"
"But she was most accommodating," said I. "She said it's fine for us to use the cottage. Here are the keys," handing them to him.
"That's very decent of her," said the Professor, taking them, "considering it belongs to me."

Tell him.

"Morag phoned," said I.
"Ah," said the Professor.
"She says she's pregnant," said I.
"Ah," said the Professor.
"She thinks you're going to marry her," said I.
"Ah," said the Professor, turning off the work station and standing up. "Shall we get going then?"
"I've decided not to come," said I. "I might as well get stuck into the cleaning. What do you want to do about all your stuff?"
"I suppose I could take it with me and sort it out up there," said the Professor.

We drove back to my flat, opened all the doors and windows, turned on the heaters and loaded the boxes into the car.

"Are you sure you won't come with me?" said the Professor, rolling up his sleeping bag.
"I'll maybe join you at the weekend," said I. "Say 'Hello' to Frances, won't you."

"Who's Francis?" said the Professor.
"The Tullybothy minister!" said I.
"Is his first name Francis?" said the Professor.

Oh.

"Are Brenda and Derek still around?" said I, casually.
"They'll not leave," said the Professor, "not with Jake just starting at Dundee. Besides, Derek's organising some international mouse mat convention. Can you imagine a hall full of mouse mat collectors?"

Derek. Jake? Frances? How long did I spend in the post box?

"What does Jake look like?" said I, tentatively.
"Very like Brenda," said the Professor, putting the bag on top of the boxes and shutting the hatchback. "It's funny though. Late one evening when we were driving back to the cottage I mistook him for you in the gloom. When I mentioned it to Julia she suddenly changed the subject. Strange eh?"
"So what about Morag?" said I.
"See you the morn, no doubt," said the Professor, getting into the car.
"On we go," said I, as he drove off.

The hall runner's ruined. I ripped it up and dumped it in the front garden. The floor boards are soaked but otherwise undamaged. I covered them with old newspapers. The front door and the walls are a mess. I'll contact the insurance company tomorrow.

Hungry. Nothing in the fridge: Pacific picnic. I shut the windows and went round the corner to the chip shop for a fish supper. Why can't they coat the haddock in bread crumbs instead of batter? Dead good chips though: outside crisp; inside soft but firm. Must be the cooking oil. Lard? On the way home, I stopped at the Co-op off-license for a six pack of Czech pils.

Back in the flat, full of warm grease and warmer beer, I discarded my temporally tarnished if calendricly fresh garb, showered and went to bed.

Out of the loop! Reflection? Summary? Conclusion? Postscript? None of the above.

Next morning, well worn routines slipped back effortlessly. By the one o'clock gun I'd had enough of shelving books and went up the hill to the sandwich bar. A cluster of tourists alighted from an open topped bus and cooed at Greyfriars Bobby.

"The usual?" said Phil, behind the counter.
"The usual," said I.
"Mushroom?" said Phil, putting an egg mayonnaise with cucumber on rye, and a ham and tomato on whole meal, into brown paper bags.
"At least it's not oxtail," said I, proffering a ten pound coin.

Cold but clear. I sat down on the bench, well in view finder range. As famous as Greyfriar's Bobby? I finished the soup and tried to decide whether to break with tradition and eat the egg before the ham.

"Fidgee fidgee?"

I looked round: the customer sat down beside me. I stared at him, mentally morphing the raw boned features.

"Felix?" said I, stunned.
"Took you long enough," said Felix.
"Why didn't you tell me?" said I.
"Because I didn't, did I," said Felix. "Not this me, or any of me I gather."

This bodes ill.

"So I'm still in transit," said I.

"'Fraid so," said Felix.

"What happens next?" said I.

"You don't know?" said Felix. "We're going to a museum."

"Can I finish my lunch first?" said I.

"Of course!" said Felix. "It doesn't open 'til two."

"Would you like something yourself?" said I.

"I'm just fine," said Felix.

Reflex conditioned, I engaged with the ham. Too much mustard. Not enough tomato.

"So why didn't Frances recognise you?" said I, brushing crumbs off my chest.

"Who's Francis?" said Felix.

"The minister in Tullybothy," said I.

"Do I know him?" said Felix.

"But I saw you there two days ago!" said I.

"Did you?" said Felix. "What was I doing?"

"Looking for Napier's bones," said I.

"That's interesting," said Felix. "How did I get there?"

"In the blue VW," said I.

"A blue VW?" said Felix, brightly. "Two days ago?"

"Didn't you know that?" said I.

"I've only just got here," said Felix.

"Haven't you used *Timeline* before?" said I.

"This is the first time," said Felix. "All I've got is this guide book."

He passed over a copy of the *Timeline Manual*. I opened the front page: my initials on the fly sheet.

Books and bones confound my clones.

"So you really don't know what's going to happen next?" said I.

"Not in any detail," said Felix. "Do you?"

"After a fashion," said I. "So how did you know where to find me?"

"She told me," said Felix. "She said you're a creature of habit."

"Which she?" said I.

"We're going to be in Tullybothy two days ago, are we," said Felix, ignoring me. "I suppose we could do that."

"We?" said I.

"You said you saw me there, didn't you?" said Felix.

"I was there already," said I.

"Was anyone there with me?" said Felix.

"Not that I noticed," said I.

"Curious!" said Felix.

"So we really haven't met before?" said I.

"You think you've met me," said Felix, "but I certainly haven't met you. Let's be off then. You're going to find this rather amusing."

I put the egg sandwich into a pocket and followed Felix: across George IVth Bridge and down Chambers Street past the old Phrenological Museum: cranialogical keystones above the windows.

I don't like this one little bit. Is he really "my" Felix? Is he really the customer? He's not after my blood. Whose blood? Which she? Robin? Her?

"What's the difference between life and skidding?" said Felix.

"I'm sure you'll tell me," said I.

"One's a vale of tears and the other's a tale of veers," said Felix.

Too clever.   ☐ By half?   ☐ For words? Mark choice with cross.

Over the road and down College Street between the National Museum and Napier University's Talbot Rice Gallery; straight across South College Street and onto Potterrow, skirting the back of the Festival Theatre, more power station than pleasure dome.

"Where are we going?" said I.
"Be patient," said Felix.

Left round Nicholson Square, over the main road and into Hill Place. Past the old Societies Centre, once the home of the Moped Rock Society. The Barnacles' first venue. My first gig. Nervous. Loud. Incompetent.

Round the corner to Hill Square and through the front door of number nine.

"This way," said Felix, taking the stairs two at a time.

On the second floor, the *Dental Museum and Sir Jules Thorn Exhibition of the History of Surgery*.

"Why are we here?" said I.
"I was assured that you'd tell me," said Felix. "In we go."

What was at first sight a tenement hall opened out at the far end into a very large room. Felix stopped at the panel opposite the entrance.

"It says we're to start here and work our way round," said Felix.
"What are we looking for?" said I.
"You'll know," said Felix.
"How's it organised?" said I.
"Chronologically of course," said Felix. "It is an history exhibition!"

I scanned the displays; desultory duty. Old surgical instruments. Old plans and deeds of medical buildings. Old limb segments in various stages of dissection. Old oils of severe looking men in wigs.

"This is a waste of time," said I.
"Keep going," said Felix.

Catheters and chancres. Battlefields and body snatchers. Anaesthesia and antiseptic.

On the far wall, a case full of brain openers. Cunning hollow hand drills for removing neat discs of bone.

A skull, crowned with a brass scold's bridle. A pointed bolt had been threaded through the forehead flange and driven through the bone into the frontal lobes. Above the bolt hole, stamped into the metal: *IN facit*.

Napier's bones?

I read the display label:

> *Trepan frame. Origin unknown. 17c?*

Followed by six familiar digits.

"Found something?" said Felix.

I pointed at the label.

"So?" said Felix.
"The acquisition code," said I. "I think that's what this is all about."
"Right," said Felix, taking out a personal organiser - expensive; Japanese; colour screen; infra-red link - and tapping at the keys. "I'll encrypt it in case

anyone else is after it."

Can a code encrypt to itself?

"Let's get going," said I. "This place is really creepy."
"Intimations of mortality," said Felix. "From the strength came forth sweetness. Besides, there are truly wonderful books here. Beautiful condition. Crammed with illustrations. Immaculate bindings."
"I'm off to the Gent's," said I.
"See you in teeth," said Felix.

I cut across the centre of the room, past the full size dissection cast and the treatment of fractures. No sign of toilets in the vestibule. Halfway up the stairs to the gallery, sounds of a scuffle below. I dashed to the top and looked down over the balustrade. Felix was struggling to his feet. A middle aged man ran from the exhibition hall. Nondescript grey suit and black raincoat. White shirt. Stripy tie, maybe a club. Clean brown shoes: always a bad sign.

"Are you all right?" I said to Felix, rejoining him in the hall.
"I'm fine," said Felix, "but the bastard's taken my organiser."
"Don't worry," said I. "He'll get his comeuppance last Thursday."
"Do I get my organiser back?" said Felix.
"I've no idea," said I.
"Where do you think he's gone?" said Felix.
"To the *Grassmarket Institute*," said I. "Or maybe he travels first. Anyway, he was dead when Robin found him. Didn't you know that? Isn't he with you lot?"
"Us lot?" said Felix. "What lot? Does it look like he's with me?"

That's hardly the point. Precisely the point.

"What now?" said I.

"Well I'm not putting up with this!" said Felix. "That's a brand new organiser! Come on!"

Felix set off down the stairs at break neck-pace. We retraced our steps to Potterrow, cut down the side of the Pill Centre, past the Men's Union, along the north side of George Square - Pharmacology, Psychology, Medical Library - and left onto Middle Meadow Walk.

"Where are we going?" said I.
"Come on!" said Felix.

At the bottom of the gentle hill, right onto North Meadow Walk.

"Where are we going!" said I.
"*Timeline Central*," said Felix.
"But there's no cemetery anywhere round here," said I.
"Cemetery?" said Felix. "I thought you'd had enough of cadavers."

Felix turned off the path onto the grass, towards the park's western apex.

"Here we are," said Felix.

I walked round the tall commemorative sundial, bending backwards to read the inscriptions on the topmost faces of the capital:

| O | TENT | TAK | TINT | BE | TIME | ERE | TIME |

"Try anti-clockwise," said Felix, studying the manual. "This side, I think."

Widdershins, I joined him under the trees.

The clouds parted. Sunshine struck the top of the pedestal. The armillary sphere began to revolve and the octagonal obelix slid slowly away from us. Golden light poured up the marble staircase.

"How did you know that would happen?" said I, amazed.
"Sheer coincidence," said Felix.
"What did you do?" said I.
"Just pressed the panel," said Felix. "Like it says in the book."
"Where are you off to?" said I.
"Last Thursday," said Felix.
"Where's your companion?" said I.

Felix looked at me.

Appendix 1

Napier's bones are an early system for simplifying multiplication. The bones are actually rectangular rods, each one inscribed with the times table for the numbers 0 to 9...

1	2	3	4	5	6	7	8	9
/1	/2	/3	/4	/5	/6	/7	/8	/9
/2	/4	/6	/8	1/0	1/2	1/4	1/6	1/8
/3	/6	/9	1/2	1/5	1/8	2/1	2/4	2/7
/4	/8	1/2	1/6	2/0	2/4	2/8	3/2	3/6
/5	1/0	1/5	2/0	2/5	3/0	3/5	4/0	4/5
/6	1/2	1/8	2/4	3/0	3/6	4/2	4/8	5/4
/7	1/4	2/1	2/8	3/5	4/2	4/9	5/6	6/3
/8	1/6	2/4	3/2	4/0	4/8	5/6	6/4	7/2
/9	1/8	2/7	3/6	4/5	5/4	6/3	7/2	8/1

... note that on each rod the column for the tens digits is separated from the column for the ones digits ... for example, consider the 4 times table rod...

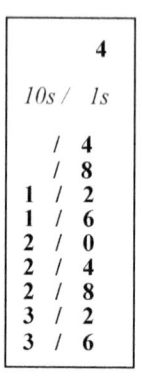

	4
10s /	1s
/	4
/	8
1 /	2
1 /	6
2 /	0
2 /	4
2 /	8
3 /	2
3 /	6

... now consider the 25 times table, which isn't one of the rods ...

$$1 * 25 = 25$$
$$2 * 25 = 50$$
$$3 * 25 = 75$$
$$4 * 25 = 100$$

... and so on ... 1 times 25 is actually 1 times 20 plus 1 times 5 ...

$$1 * 25 => 1 * 20 + 1 * 5 => 20 + 5$$

... 2 times 25 is 2 times 20 plus 2 times ...

$$2 * 25 => 2 * 20 + 2 * 5 => 40 + 10$$

... 3 times 25 is 3 times 20 plus 3 times 5 ...

$$3 * 25 => 3 * 20 + 3 * 5 => 60 + 15$$

...and so on .. .so we can work out the 25 times table if we know the 20 times table and the 5 times table ... of course, the 20 times table is just 10 times the 2 times table ...

$$1 * 20 = 20 = 10 * 1 * 2$$
$$2 * 20 = 40 = 10 * 2 * 2$$
$$3 * 20 = 60 = 10 * 3 * 2$$

... and so on ... now let's look at the rods for 2 and 5 again, put together as if they were one rod for 25 ...

	10s			1s		
	2			5		
	100s / 10s			10s / 1s		
		/	2		/	5
		/	4	1	/	0
		/	6	1	/	5
		/	8	2	/	0
	1	/	0	2	/	5
	1	/	2	3	/	0
	1	/	4	3	/	5
	1	/	6	4	/	0
	1	/	8	4	/	5

… the rod for 2 is in the tens position so now it shows the 20 times table … the tens digits on the 2's rod are now hundreds digits and the ones digits on the 2's rod are now tens digits … the rod for 5 is in the ones position so its still the 5 times table … its tens digits are still tens digits and its one digits are still ones digits … now let's label each row …

	10s			1s		
	2			5		
	100s / 10s			10s / 1s		
1		/	2		/	5
2		/	4	1	/	0
3		/	6	1	/	5
4		/	8	2	/	0
5	1	/	0	2	/	5
6	1	/	2	3	/	0
7	1	/	4	3	/	5
8	1	/	6	4	/	0
9	1	/	8	4	/	5

…the first row is 1 times 25, that is a 2 in the tens position from the 2's rod plus a 5 in the ones position from the 5's rod which is 20 plus 5 which is 25…

... the second row is 2 times 25, that is a 4 in the tens position from the 2's rod plus a 1 in the tens position from the 5's rod plus a 0 in the ones position from the 5's rod which is 40 plus 10 plus 0 which is 50...

...the third row is 3 times 25, that is a 6 in the tens position from the 2's rod plus a 1 in the tens position from the 5's rod plus a 5 in the ones position from the 5's rod which is 60 plus 10 plus 5 which is 75...

Appendix 2

TIMELINE

FOR THE BEST OF ALL POSSIBLE WORLDS!
Tak tent o time ere time be tint.

SOME MYTHS DISPELLED
TIMELINE is not:
- time travel
- faster than light
- perpetual motion
- matter transference
- replication
- magic

HOW DOES IT WORK?
TIMELINE is based on everyday quantum physics. Reality is the expression of one of a fantastically large number of equally probable superimposed states. When you specify a desired state, *TIMELINE* determines the minimum number of changes to reach it from your initial state.

TIMELINE then generates a sequence of minute transitions from your initial state to your desired state. Each transition takes a very small but nonetheless positive amount of energy. The number of transitions between your initial and desired states is astronomically large. Thus, the total energy required to reach your desired state is incomprehensibly enormous. Consequently, with steady but economic energy expenditure, it usually takes an astonishingly long time to effect the sequence of transitions.

HOW WILL IT AFFECT ME?

TIMELINE guarantees that the transition to your desired state will appear to you to be almost instantaneous. Your memories of your life before using the service will be substantially unaltered. You will not experience any extreme dislocation, fatigue or jet-lag. Coherent gross change on a large scale is vanishingly improbable. Moreover, any change to yourself will be minimised.

CAN I AFFORD IT?

Everyone can afford *TIMELINE*! A very reasonable one-off payment is invested for your required period of state transition. This covers all costs.

HOW ACCURATE IS TIMELINE?

A full description of a given state of reality would take all of reality to represent! Consequently, *TIMELINE* is based on calculating local differences between states which may introduce minuscule rounding errors. While such errors tend to cancel out across a long sequence of transitions, *TIMELINE* is a probabilistic process. Thus, *TIMELINE* necessarily cannot guarantee 100% precision. For small transitions, very high accuracy is normal. For larger transitions, however, there may be some minor temporal/spatial drift.

WHAT CAN I TAKE WITH ME?

TIMELINE can reliably transport anything in direct physical contact with you, for example your clothing and jewellery. Anything else you want to take must also be in direct contact with you, for example in a pocket or in a bag on your back or held in your hand. There is a very low probability of any significant change to such immediate possessions. However, anything not in direct contact with you may well not arrive at the same place and time. *TIMELINE* also offers a send and trace service. For further details, please call our Information Hotline.

WARNING

It is important to note that *TIMELINE* services are probably irreversible.

It is also important to note that the repeated use of *TIMELINE* services may result in cumulative physiological effects.

TIMELINE and their authorised agents cannot accept any

responsibility for the consequences of service use.

SERVICE DIRECTORY

The following sections tell you all about:
- the full range of *TIMELINE* services
- how to locate your nearest *TIMELINE* facility
- how to use your selected *TIMELINE* service, step by step
- how to contact the *TIMELINE* Information Hotline
- full prices of all *TIMELINE* services
- payment methods ...

Acknowledgements

- p5: Iona & Peter Opie, *The Oxford Nursery Rhyme Book*, Oxford, 1955.
- p20: Richard Dawkins, *River Out of Eden*, Basic Books, 1995.
- p54: Oscar Wilde, *The Ballad of Reading Goal*, Phoenix, 1996.
- p120: Herbert Read, *The Green Child*, Penguin, 1969.
- p126 & 127: William Shakespeare, *The Tempest*, Signet, 1964.
- p172: Anon, *The First Book of Moses, called Genesis*, in *The Holy Bible*, Scottish Bible Society, 1958.
- p173: Anon, *The Gospel According to St Mark*, in *The Holy Bible*, Scottish Bible Society, 1958.
- p178: Mark Twain, *The Mysterious Stranger*, in *The Mysterious Stranger and Other Stories*, Dover, 1992.

I'd like to thank:
- Andrew Cook, Michael Grant and Jan Natanson for comments on early drafts of *Napier's Bones*;
- Wilma Alexander, for her customary thoroughness in rooting out myriad mistakes;
- Brendan Gisby for giving *Napier's Bones* such a good home.

I'd particularly like to thank Nancy Falchikov, always my stalwart companion.

Front cover: frontispiece of Cave Beck's *Universal Character* (author's collection).

Printed in Great Britain
by Amazon